# Sleight of Hand

Elizabeth Wassell was born in Manhattan, and studied fiction writing with Grace Paley and Edna O'Brien. She has worked as a restaurant critic, a barmaid, an English lecturer and a public relations writer. Having travelled and lived extensively in Europe, particularly England and Ireland, she has now settled in West Cork. Her acclaimed first novel, *The Honey Plain* — the first novel written about Irish summer schools — was published in 1997.

*For Ruth, Emily, Allison and Melissa*

## ALSO BY ELIZABETH WASSELL

*The Honey Plain*
(Wolfhound, 1997)

# Sleight of Hand

## Elizabeth Wassell

WOLFHOUND PRESS
Celebrating 25 Years

First published in 1999 by
Wolfhound Press Ltd
68 Mountjoy Square
Dublin 1
Ireland

 Wolfhound Press receives financial assistance from The Arts Council/An Chomhairle Ealaíon, Dublin, Ireland.

British Library Cataloguing in Publication Data
A catalogue record for this book is available from the British Library.

The author gratefully acknowledges the permission of Michael Longley to reproduce the poem 'Narcissus' from his collection *No Continuing City*, © Michael Longley, 1969, and of John O'Leary to reproduce the poem 'Echo', unpublished.

ISBN 0-86327-733-0

Cover Design: Slick Fish Design, Dublin
Cover Illustration: Orla Gilbourne
Typesetting: Wolfhound Press
Printed in Ireland by Colour Books, Dublin

# Part One

Unweatherbeaten as the moon my face
Among the waterlogged, the commonplace,

Old boots and kettles for inheritance
Drifting into my head on the off-chance —

A wide Sargasso where the names of things
(Important guests at all such christenings)

Submerge in mind and pool like treasure-trove.
My face as sole survivor floats above.

'Narcissus'
Michael Longley

*Downtown Manhattan, the late 1980s*

# Prologue

Simon dragged the brush down the canvas, producing a plank of colour, green-gold. Then he narrowed his eyes, but felt nothing; it was only a panel of pigment on the dead, white, reproachful canvas. He made a sibilant noise, a hiss of frustration and disgust.

Once, the brushes in his strict hand had yielded such light! Emerald, cobalt, white hard as chalk, lush as cream or blue as milk. Magenta, fiery orange-red, cold blue-red, sullen violets, the teal colour of dreaming. But now light and colour eluded him, and his attempts at composition were pathetic; no tension or mystery. He threw down the brush as though it had burnt him.

Walking over to the window, he looked out at SoHo, at the black iron vines scrolled across an ornate building, once a factory, now converted into galleries and studios – and lofts like his own. At least the Italian social club was still down there, just across the street. The local gangsters still assembled in it, daily, to settle their elbows on white tablecloths rough from many launderings, to gaze lugubriously at the TV, drink colourless *grappa*, and talk business. But soon it would go too, he was sure. Soon SoHo would be nothing but pretentious art galleries, hip restaurants, and expensive boutiques, fake as Montmartre, not an old-fashioned criminal in sight.

He lit a cigarette, and gazed abstractedly at the bright sky. He was thinking that since he couldn't release his tensions onto the canvas today, he would walk over to Fanelli's and at least paint his morning red.

\* \* \*

At such an early hour Fanelli's was nearly empty, and so dim that the sunlight smoked in through its old windows. Simon ordered a whiskey; then, suddenly, while he was idly listening to the clash and rumble of trucks along Prince Street, a tremor of joy flared through him.

The barman's hand on the counter, a newspaper furled on one of the tables, the waitress's long hair, all were suffused with a kind of brightness. He could not fathom it, could only conclude that the source of this joy must be something in himself, something lost or forgotten, but which for some reason had quickened now, at this ordinary moment, and during one of his blue periods, no less! Swallowing his drink, he said to himself that he must not give up; tomorrow he would paint again.

At that moment a burly man with wild grey eyebrows sidled up next to him. 'Mr Simon Brady?' he cried in a German accent, grinning delightedly. 'Ah, I know who you are. Please, let me buy you another drink.'

Bemused, Simon looked up from his whiskey: his bliss had vanished, but he would remember it, he would remember. Lightheaded and vulnerable, he could detect no menace in the flushed face before him. 'Yes,' he answered, 'Yes, of course, thank you.' The German, no doubt a collector, proceeded to talk animatedly about galleries, dealers, and fashionable artists, and by their next whiskey Simon had decided that the fellow was pleasant enough, though slightly sardonic with his bitter smile and those eyebrows that moved up and down like demented caterpillars – anyway he would serve to pass the time until Simon got back to work.

But then, after yet another drink, the tone changed. The man suddenly gave a low, ugly laugh and cried in his harsh accent, 'Ah, yes, the great Simon Brady! Simon Brady, the *genius*. A few years ago you were so famous for your colour-field abstraction canvases. Yes, I remember! I believe one critic called you the most important painter of the decade. He actually compared you to Monet! How fulsome they are, the critics, don't you agree? And of course you and I know the truth, do we not? You created those pictures by spraying paint onto a canvas from an aerosol canister, the way people kill flies. What a good joke, what fun, dear Mr Brady! Your colour-field paintings bear about as much resemblance to Monet as a roll of toilet paper does to an illuminated manu-script! Ah, yes, I must congratulate you. We all know that contemporary art is a con job. But so far only you have had the guts to beat them at their own game!'

Simon, to his disbelief (so seriously had he underestimated his own rage and disappointment) heard himself scream, 'You dumb Kraut! Go shove a *bratwurst* up your ass! You wouldn't know the difference between a painting and a pickled pig's foot! Take that, you Hun!' And he poured the lees of his whiskey over the man's head before seizing his overcoat and bolting from the bar, his hand still shaking.

# Chapter One

Long ago Simon had noticed that at night the buildings of SoHo gleamed silver. It was uncanny to him, a young, hungry painter taking nocturnal rambles along Spring Street, King Street, Mercer and Grand, lost in his dream. And the buildings themselves had seemed to be dreaming; still, at that time, largely undiscovered by the artists and dealers who would later transform them, first into a bohemian colony, then a commercial Mecca.

Later he read, or someone might have told him, that the old SoHo warehouses glowed in this way because they were made not of stone, but of iron, with its lustrous patina. And Simon, while satisfied with this reasonable explanation, still remembered his early dream of a SoHo grim and sooty by day, but, at night, flushed with an inner radiance, strange as quicksilver.

It had never occurred to him during that distant, restive period that he might be in danger, walking alone down pavements where cats prowled, past silent Italian food shops smelling vaguely of cheese and spices. He had loved the vast warehouses with their elaborate lintels and Grecian friezes, to which the ubiquitous fire-escapes clung like spiders. In those early years SoHo (not even yet called SoHo) was still an industrial area, largely empty after dusk except for the black-swathed grandmothers and noisy children of Italian MacDougal Street. The few people he would sometimes pass – a tense prostitute, a grizzled man on some stealthy mission – would give him a puzzled glance. He must have seemed strange to them, an intent young man with a pale Irish face and paint in his hair, walking alone in the darkness.

Ah, but he had travelled far from that young man's romantic dream. In the early, mercenary eighties, when he finally became successful, the only white light in his life were the flares in his head, the white-hot brain explosions ignited by cocaine. Jesus, those parties: the membranes of his nose seared and raw, artists and patrons and wheeler-dealers crouching on varnished floors with furled-up one-hundred-dollar bills pushed up their nostrils, their elegant lofts a squalid mess by dawn. They swilled champagne and snorted coke all night, emerged from restaurant toilets gabbling feverishly while the haute cuisine grew cold on their plates, seethed through the clubs dressed in ultra-cool black, till morning broke, cruel and strident, and their vials were empty.

Well, coke was going out of fashion now, and in recent years Simon hadn't done it at all. Then his pal Owen Kettlethorpe, a well-known art expert, arrived unexpectedly one Sunday in

December; he had just flown in from London with a cache of duty-free booze and a gram of cocaine concealed in a bottle of laxatives. It was two in the afternoon when they began drinking the liquor and snorting the coke, and before long they were babbling clichés in urgent voices and laughing with astonished glee at their own intelligence. And since Owen was also addled by the time change, his behaviour was especially febrile.

'Simon,' he cried at one point, waving his arms, 'What's wrong? What's up? You look *terrible.*'

'Can't work. Can't paint. Lost my touch,' Simon answered, taking a self-pitying slurp of duty-free whiskey. It was just after the incident at Fanelli's with the bellicose German, and he was feeling exceptionally discouraged. His brief high in the bar had evaporated and had never come back.

Owen began chopping up more cocaine with a razor blade. 'Oh, Simon, it's a strange world in SoHo these days. Even the most negligible artist can make a name for himself if he has enough chutzpah and the right connections, and if his work is bizarre or splashy or large enough. And my *confrères*, the so-called experts, certainly don't help. They can't tell the ersatz from the real, most of them. And their mumbo-jumbo! They don't think, or feel, for themselves, you know. Here, have another blast of whiskey.'

Simon regarded his friend affectionately. Owen was a gangly man with silver hair, rough, handsome features and a courtly manner. Though born in Tulsa he had lived in London for the past twenty years, with a succession of women all as willowy and elegant as himself. His family was oil-rich, and a look of wealth clung to him, a kind of sheen. Simon, emboldened by whiskey and coke, suddenly asked, 'Owen, have you ever authenticated a painting you knew was fake? Maybe just to give yourself a laugh at the expense of the experts? After all, *they're* the real fakes.'

Owen looked slyly at him. 'Of course not. Heaven forbid! But I must admit that at times I have indulged in a bit of harmless mischief. Last month, in fact, I deliberately confused a particularly annoying curator, just to give myself the bitter satisfaction of seeing him behave like the sycophant he is, agreeing with every fulsome thing I said about an actually quite inferior minor Baroque work. Here, take some more of this stuff before I hoover it all up myself.'

They went on to talk more about modern art, and the Baroque period, which was Owen's area of expertise, especially the Spanish Baroque: Ribera, Velasquez, Moreno. Then they talked about women in general, and one in particular.

'Has Derby mentioned this girl, Claire, to you?' Simon asked. 'I'm thinking of taking her on to sort out my papers.' Darby Holland, an art historian who worked at *ArtDimension* magazine, had recently told Simon about one of his colleagues, a girl who wrote art history articles for the magazine. She intrigued Darby because she was curiously naïve, even childish, despite having been born in New York and living in the louche East Village. Darby had said that before meeting her he'd expected this girl to be a hip downtown type, but instead she appeared to move in a dream, to glide through her days like a creature from some other century. According to Darby she was not beautiful, but softly pretty in a way that old-fashioned novels invariably describe as 'fetching', a little Victorian heroine. She sometimes exasperated him, Darby had explained, because it was hard to believe that such wide-eyed innocence could be completely guileless, especially since this woman lived close to Alphabet City, surrounded by poverty, homelessness, violence, drugs, and the ethnic tensions which smouldered among the Latinos, Blacks, and eastern Europeans of Avenues B, C, and D. But despite her naïveté Darby was fond of her, in a non-sexual way, and had recommended this girl, called Claire something-or-other, to Simon.

Owen gave Simon a hard look. 'To organise your papers? Are you imagining that this young woman might help you recover your lost touch?'

'God, no.' Simon sighed irritably. 'I've lost my touch because I'm bitter and disgusted. I just can't stomach the art biz any more, and I can't stomach myself either, my self-betrayals. And despite what you're implying, you old wolf, I really don't think that an ill-considered affair with Darby's mascot would be a good idea just now.' He paused. 'But, you know, I have been wanting to paint the figure again. And I haven't had a good model for ages. So it's strange, I some-times think of her, this girl with the cameo face and dreamy expression, the way Darby describes her. And I think maybe I would like to paint someone who looks like that, because I've been feeling so disaffected lately, and such a model, such gentleness, could be a kind of antidote or something, a tonic for my bitterness.'

He laughed in a slightly shamefaced way. 'I used to love to use that beautiful Puerto Rican model, remember? Her face was all hard planes. And Olivia's face was similar, so *angular*. But now, as I said, the idea of softness... I don't know. Any-way, that Harvard scholar who writes biographies of artists has approached me. She wants to read my correspondence and papers, which are a real mess. I don't want to go through them all myself, all those letters and photographs and books. It would be too overwhelming, excavating myself like some broken-down civilisation.'

Owen, touching his reddened nose with a tissue, reflected, 'I think I might know who she is, this girl of Darby's. There *is* a young woman called Claire something – Browne, I think – who has written pieces on the Spanish Baroque for *Art-Dimension*. They are quite good, actually. It really must be the same girl. She called me once, asking for some information about Ribera, I believe, his period in Naples or something. A bright young woman.'

Simon walked over to the window. It was dusk, and the streetlamps had just come on. The sky was lilac over the restless city, recalling to Simon other, older twilights: that same vaporous lilac glow over home in Gloucester, Massachusetts, the sounds of doors closing in the distance, mothers calling to children, lamps burning in curtained rooms, and boredom, sadness, longing. Now he thought, Soon it will be night, the glassy darkness of New York in winter. He closed the curtains and turned on the lights.

When he returned to the sofa Owen was doing still more coke, and talking fast. 'I can't understand why Darby bothers to write for *ArtDimension*. That magazine is so trendy and self-important. But they've given you some good reviews, Simon.'

'Some bad ones, too, depending on the fashion. Oh, Jesus, sometimes I think I've dreamt my life.' He tried to explain what he meant, that in the sixties and seventies he'd seen no evidence, registered no signals, that the world would change as quickly as it had done. How had the eighties happened? Where, for instance, had the yuppies come from? All these ruthless young people, old before their time, trafficking in

Money and Power and Image, people for whom the life of the spirit, the love of books and paintings, the idea of social responsibility, meant nothing, less than nothing. But why had he never seen them coming?

'Is that why you are intrigued by this mythical art history girl of Darby's?' Owen interrupted, 'After all, she doesn't sound like a product of the eighties. She sounds like someone who lives in her own dream world.'

Simon was silent a moment. 'I think my marriage failed partly because I had always had this horror of family life, of any kind of settled routine. I imagined suburban towns full of dull couples with screaming children, their whole lives defined by mortgages and television and supermarkets, that sort of thing, and it appalled me. So I was scared of settling down, and I liked it when I became famous and a lot of girls were suddenly throwing themselves at me. Poor Olivia! But now my life has changed, and the possibility of love, just a good, gentle love, is not so unattractive. Only I'm not thinking of this girl for that role. She works for *ArtDimension*, which, as you said, is a pretentious rag, and for all I know she's pretentious, too. On the other hand, if she really is as naïve and innocent as Darby says – Jesus! I'm too old and tired to get involved with anything like that.'

Owen suddenly gulped down his whiskey, and replenished his glass. 'Simon,' he said in a low, excited voice, 'Simon. A thought just occurred to me. Perhaps it's the coke, I don't know. But something about this girl, her naïveté, and how you were just describing the current art scene, and the pretentious critics who write for *ArtDimension*... I might be mad, Simon, but listen. Just listen. I think I have a scheme that will amuse us both, for a long time.'

# Chapter Two

*M*en surged her into the downtown local, where the air was thick with wool, chemical heat, souring cologne. And a phantom intimacy. She was surrounded entirely by men: two burly fellows in identical green boiler suits; a man with flowing hair and a lean, Pre-Raphaelite face; a school-teacher, probably, wearing glasses and clutching a satchel full of papers; businessmen; paranoid schizophrenics; her underground companions, crushed against her, embracing her, enfolding her with an inadvertent tenderness.

She regarded their hands: tapering, blunt, square, spatulate, callused, seamed, smooth, furry, coffee-coloured, pink, black – and all these hands began to kindle a vague thrill of desire in her when, suddenly, she felt one on her left leg.

At first she thought it might be a fantasy, conjured up

*from her reverie, but the hand was definitely there, gliding slowly up her thigh; she could feel it, heavy and warm, through the light mesh of her stocking. She eased away from it, closer against the schoolteacher. He smiled politely at her, his eyes blue-grey.*

*But she had not evaded the hand; stealthily, it returned, and continued its slow progress upwards along her thigh. To whom did it belong? And how could it be so audacious, touching her intimately in front of everyone on the downtown local? And what was* she *feeling? Repugnance, indignation, terror, lust, as those deliberate fingers moved up and up? Then, abruptly, they stopped, on her inner thigh, and reposed there, in neutral country. So, she thought, he's lost his nerve. She wondered whose hand it could be; a lonely old man's? She tried to picture him: grey, small, desperately shy; pictured his apartment: a tenement building, a maroon sheet curtaining the one sooty window, a mess of dishes on the stove, a narrow bed like a monk's pallet. He did nothing all day but sprawl on that bed, listening to the radio and staring up at the distempered ceiling, till five o'clock, when he descended into these depths and went about his furtive business. And if right now he were to thrust that hand of his down into her underpants, what would she do? Would her excited flesh thrash and dissolve against his fingers? Would she scream? Or remain perfectly still, gazing blandly ahead into the grey eyes of the schoolteacher?*

The local stopped at Astor Place, her station, and she left, carried out on the current of men. Then suddenly it was a spring evening, sunlight fading in the sky. Claire smoothed a hand over her face. The dream still clung in her memory, vivid yet obscure, like an old blue movie. She could still feel the carriage shuddering beneath her feet, see the schoolteacher's satchel bulging with papers, but the emotions which lingered now were shame and fear, though she didn't know why. Then, for a fraction of a second, before it was absorbed into that deep place where dreams are cargoed during the day, she remembered the hand, but the image dissolved before her mind could fasten on it, and she was left with the evening. And with the knowledge that she was going to her parents' sad apartment for dinner and that her father, once a brilliant biology professor, was now ailing, dying.

\* \* \*

Claire's parents had lived for thirty-five years in an art deco building on Central Park West. Claire herself had been born in a tall, oyster-coloured, art deco hospital on York Avenue. She had always liked New York's art deco buildings, their balance of weight and light, their stone crescents, how they thrust their spires into the sky like cathedrals, even though they celebrated not saints, but commerce: The Chrysler, The Woolworth.

At half-past seven she emerged from the IND station and walked north along the park's border, where the trees threw ragged shadows out of which a squirrel jumped, suddenly, making her gasp.

When she arrived at her parents' door her mother drew her in and with a quaver said, 'I told your father you were coming, but he won't move. He's–'

'Where is he?'

'In bed, still. I've been trying to get him up, but...'

'Why don't I go in and see what I can do?'

She opened the door of her parents' bedroom. As a child,

20

during the long day when her parents were at work, she had always taken a voluptuous pleasure in entering this room, pleasure in its perfumed darkness after the bright street, the way outdoor noises were abruptly muffled here among her mother and father's things: the mirror, the photograph of her grandfather, the ceramic bowl full of bracelets and rings, her father's dresser onto which every evening he divested himself of his daytime burdens: wallet, coins, handkerchief. Sometimes when she walked through this room she could hear no sounds at all – the air would be soaked in an odd silence composed of shadow and dry sunlight, the glinting faces of clocks, and a smell of cooking from the apartment next door – like the charged expectancy of certain Vermeers. In the evening it was different: the din of the TV, her mother's clothes and her father's newspapers thrown on the bed, and often the whiskey or vodka bottle among her mother's scarves and earrings under the mirror, with a smeared glass beside it. Now the room was dark.

'Dad?' she called.

'Claire-Bear?' His voice came from the bed.

As her eyes adjusted to the gloom, she saw him reclining on his back, stiff as a tomb effigy, his hands cupped over his chest, fully dressed except for his shoes. Her mother had told her that lately he'd begun sleeping a great deal during the day. Earlier on in the course of his affliction, when he could no longer read, the television had offered him some vague distraction, but now when he switched it on and saw a woman sobbing or cowboys battling, he himself would weep or cry out in fear. So were his days narrowing, their loneliness deepening, and he slept, and Claire wondered what he dreamt. His conscious life had become so like a dream; the pleats and puckers of time, all his past and present, sprawled out before him now like a vast fogbound plain, through which he moved with no lamp to guide him. He spoke to his dead father, mistook Claire for his grandmother, believed himself back in his mother's house.

A man living among shades, what could sleep be like for him now, how did he travel in that region where no-one is harnessed to ordinary time, where the dead come alive for us all? Could sleep be his last refuge, Claire sometimes wondered. Did the shades greet him at the portal of dreams, their arms extended, to say, Don't be afraid. Here there is no pressure. We are all the same here. There is no such thing as time... She also sometimes imagined that at the moment of his return from sleep, at the precise moment his eyes opened, there was a second of clarity before the sickness closed in again. But of course that wasn't possible.

'Daddy?' She settled softly down next to him and touched his hand. 'I've come to visit, to see you.'

'Is that Claire?' His eyes, immense and stricken, moved from the ceiling to her face. 'I want to go home,' he said simply.

She answered evenly. 'You are home, Daddy. Look. This is your room.'

Slowly he regarded walls, furniture, shadow-pooled corners; then brought his hands up to his face and examined them, backs and palms. She registered that while his face had lost flesh and his eyes their lustre, his hands were still the same. Lowering them, he asked, 'Where is my mother?'

Claire paused. Then she took his hand in both her own. How heavy and strong it was, with its dry palm and long fingers. She answered gently, 'Grandmother Fabienne died, Daddy, seven years ago.'

'Died?' His dark eyes – her own eyes – surveyed her warily.

Trying to keep her voice steady she went on, 'Remember? She told us that she didn't mind dying, because she was so weary, and had had such a good, long life.'

Suddenly, like canvases toppling, his face collapsed on itself and he began to cry, piteously, like a child. 'No,' he sobbed, 'It can't be true. When did she die? Why didn't you tell me?'

Claire thought this was one of the most merciless aspects of his disease, how it threw him continually against old sorrows as though they were fresh. With the dismantling of his memory he was shocked by grief again and again; his loved ones died every day, ten times a day, always a first blow, always these startled eyes and rasping tears. She kept his hand in hers and willed him to forget, again.

After a few minutes she prevailed on him to come out into the living room, where her mother was anxiously waiting beside the coffee table on which she had arranged drinks and a plate of crudités. This attempt at festivity – the good wine glasses, the bright carrots and radishes – brought Claire herself nearly to tears. She said with stilted jauntiness, 'Here's Dad. I've lured him out of bed.' And to her father, 'Come, Daddy, onto the sofa.'

'Why?' He answered petulantly, 'I don't want to. I want to go for a walk.'

Her mother said, 'Gerald, dear, you can't go for a walk. It's too late. Besides, darling, dinner is ready. I've cooked dinner for us. Claire has come over tonight for *dinner*.'

'Where are my shoes?' He looked grimly at Claire. 'Cecily takes my shoes so I can't leave. And my money. Look,' he pointed to his feet, 'You can see for yourself what she does.'

Claire tried to give her mother a comforting smile. Poor Cecily, wringing her hands over the nice hors d'oeuvres and glasses of wine she had prepared with special care. How earnestly she still tried to make things seem pleasant! Claire said hurriedly, 'Dad, my friend Zoë wanted you to know she was awfully sorry she couldn't come tonight.'

Her father looked in puzzlement at Claire and murmured, 'Zoë? My colleague at the university, isn't she? I haven't seen her for a long time.' Tractable now, he let her ease him onto the sofa.

'This particular Zoë is my neighbour, down in the East Village where I live. Here, Dad, have a glass of apple juice.' He was not permitted alcohol any more.

Cecily gave her a grateful look. They were all three silent for a while. The lamplight-flushed curtains, the throb of traffic from below, the smells of roast beef and baked potatoes, reminded Claire that as a child she had looked forward every day to the moment when her father would come home from the university, breathing into this close domestic place his masculine fragrances of leather and tobacco, taking her in his arms and pressing his cheek, cold with the savour of outdoors, against her warm one. Now her mother asked, 'So, tell us about this new job you are applying for.'

Claire immediately smelled trouble. Her mother had always been hungrily dependent (due to what ancient wound or betrayal Claire did not know), and since her husband's illness she had, quite naturally, become more demanding and unreasonable than ever. These days, any news concerning her daughter's independent life was usually welcomed sullenly, querulously, or with tears. Claire felt herself recoil physically, as though her mother were actually clutching her or breathing greedily into her face. Her own life, still young, clamoured for her attention: this possible new job with the painter Simon Brady; her desire to write a book about Caravaggio, to travel, to drink wine in a café, glancing out at ancient houses drowsing in the heat of afternoon, to visit the Louvre, the Prado, the Tate, to discover love. Life, her own life, called to her, and with the natural selfishness of youth she recoiled from the sadness in this house, and from her mother whose hunger was so ruthless.

She said, 'It's a simple job. My friend, Darby Holland, who works with me at *ArtDimension*, told me about it. Some woman is doing a biography of Simon Brady, and he needs help to organise his papers and correspondence for her.'

Claire's father shambled to his feet and began walking towards the kitchen. Claire made to follow but her mother said, 'Let him go; he needs to potter. And when he cleans up and moves things around he feels he's being helpful.' She frowned. 'But Claire, are you saying that you are applying to be this man's *secretary*? With your degree in art history, and those lovely articles you write? What could possibly attract you to such tedious work?' She made a pout of disapproval. 'Besides, if the job takes up too much of your day, you won't be available if I need you.'

Swallowing, Claire prepared to speak, when suddenly Cecily gave a shout, jumped to her feet, and bolted towards the bathroom. For a second Claire stared after her; then she heard it, the roar of an outraged toilet. *Jesus*, she thought, and hurried after her mother into the small lavatory where her father, the kitchen rubbish basket dangling from his hand, was looking fixedly into the overflowing bowl. Water surged out from it, cascading onto the floor, and borne on the spill were bedraggled celery leaves, coffee grounds, chicken bones, orange rinds, and other lumps of kitchen garbage too sodden to recognise. Cecily shrieked, 'He's emptied the bin into the toilet, the toilet, the toilet!' Claire's father said calmly, 'See the water.'

Crouching so that the curdled water, a banana skin, and two bleached bones were sloshing against her calves, Claire wrenched at the red wheel on the wall underneath the basin. Immediately the flow ceased, and she had a brief sensation of the room listing and then righting itself like a boat. Her mother hadn't stopped screaming and now she was clutching at her hair in a manner Claire couldn't but consider cartoonishly melodramatic. Jews! she thought exasperatedly, temporarily allying herself with her father's genteel Protestant family, and choosing, conveniently, to forget her own turmoil.

'Mom,' she commanded, 'Control yourself. Everything's all right now. Come, you're upsetting Dad.'

Cecily glared at her. 'Look at this!' She threw out her arms, indicating the turbid water, soggy rubbish, and the toilet smeared with a greenish froth and clumps of what looked like scrambled egg. 'Upsetting Dad? Upsetting Dad? Just look at this disgusting mess! Who do you think will have to clean it up?' She burst into noisy tears.

Gerald's eyes were huge and staring. 'See,' he cried with bitter triumph, 'See how she humiliates me!'

'Daddy, Mom,' Claire implored, 'let's get out of here.' The water was lapping greasily at their ankles. To her mother she said, 'Elvis will repair the toilet, and help us clean up.' Elvis was the superintendent, who had worked in this building for over thirty years, and who still rumpled Claire's hair whenever he saw her, as though she had never stopped being a child scurrying home after a day in Central Park.

Her father said, 'Claire, what's wrong with Cecily? Where is she? What did I do?'

'Fuck!' bellowed Cecily from the kitchen, 'I've lost Elvis's phone number!'

Gerald's eyes widened further. In a keening, terrified voice he cried, 'Don't be angry with me! I didn't do anything wrong! I didn't do anything!'

Claire threw her arms around him. 'Of course you didn't, Daddy. Everything's fine, really it is.'

He drew back. 'What is wrong with your mother? Did you upset her? What did you do to upset her?' He staggered up and into the kitchen. Claire followed, to see her mother sobbing angrily among a riot of pots, dishes, and a rosy roast beef on a platter.

'That beef doesn't look overcooked,' Claire said soothingly. 'It looks all pink and nice.'

'I can't take this anymore!' Cecily's face was mottled red and white. She brandished a serving spoon at Claire. 'Why should *you* care? You're never *here*, you don't know what it's like to live in this house day after day, you almost never come to see us, you'd rather tidy up bits of paper for some abstract artist than visit your poor father, you selfish *bitch*!'

Claire tried to speak but something was sticking in her throat. Finally she said, 'What would you have me do? Give up my life?'

Cecily cried, 'He's driving me–'

'Quiet, Mom, please! You can be *heard!* Shut up!'

Her father roared, 'Claire, stop upsetting your mother!' Claire whirled around and saw him glowering at her; in a detached way she noticed that although she had inherited the brunette colour of his eyes, hers were not moulded like his. His eyes had rough straight lashes and bulged slightly, while her own and her mother's were wide spaced. She looked from him to Cecily; both their faces were contorted with rage, and for a brief white moment she hated them both.

Then her mother buried her head in her hands and began to cry, and her father to lament, 'But what did I do? What did I do?' And Claire, overcome with pity, with anger, with the bile of old grievances, closed her eyes, threw back her head, and silently screamed, a large-eyed Munch figure standing on a bridge of sighs.

# Chapter Three

Simon took a gulp of tepid coffee from the cup balanced precariously on his paint-encrusted work table. Also on the table, beside a bottle of flaring brushes, was this week's *ArtDimension*. He eyed it warily, as though the hateful review were literally smouldering in its pages, ready to ignite at any moment. Although he wanted to fire the magazine through the window, flush it down the toilet, incinerate it, he accepted ruefully that what he would doubtless do instead was the most stubborn, foolish, and ill-advised thing possible: he'd read the review again and again until he had memorised each one of its vacuous, vicious phrases; he would relish his bitterness as though it were joy; he would stew in his own disaffected juice.

Sighing, he seized the magazine and brought it with his

coffee over to the sofa. *Luke Reilly Takes SoHo By Storm*, he read. Then:

'Reilly's exhibition at SoHo's prestigious Carlyle Gallery constitutes a dazzling departure for the young painter. These new canvasses evoke the work of Simon Brady, but Reilly's paintings are much more daring than any of Brady's recent efforts, which strike one as dismayingly cold and superficial, suggesting no mysteries beneath their arid candor. Brady's quality of controlled neutrality might have startled us in the Pop days, but now it seems far from fresh. Luke Reilly, on the other hand, appears to be venturing into new and compelling aesthetic territory...'

Simon took another irritable slurp of coffee. How could even a magazine as phoney as *ArtDimension* permit this critic, this Brian Solonik, to foul its pages with such affected rubbish? 'Prestigious Carlyle Gallery' indeed: it was only a tarted-up hole in the wall, managed by a nasty *tapette*. And gibberish like 'dazzling departure', 'arid candor', 'new and compelling aesthetic territory'! Brian Solonik, whoever he was, must be the most insufferable sycophant in all New York. And the hogwash he wrote didn't *mean* anything, it was just the drivel these people spouted so capriciously, as though art, and artists' lives, meant nothing. Owen had been right when he had declared it so ironical that these pretentious critics should regard themselves as the keepers of the flame! They, who soiled art with their passionless and false phrases, who made kings and then toppled them, who were driven by nothing more than the desire to promote themselves. Why, everyone knew that Luke Reilly was really just a talentless huckster, an arrogant pipsqueak. But his new gimmick, 'fermented food paintings' (composed of acrylic pigments and cheeses which sprouted mould and fur as the canvases aged), was considered super-cool. Simon threw the magazine to the floor. One could only conclude that art was no longer real; it was real estate, and the genuine effort of some lonely man or woman to actually *create*, to *break through*, had been rendered ludicrous.

He finished his coffee, which had taken on a faint flavour of turpentine. He'd never understood any of it, even the accolades they used to give his own work. One critic had praised his last exhibition as 'quivering with fragile emotion which refines the artistic *weltschmerz* to a new pitch while exploring the foibles of our human drama.' Gobbledygook! If they had just written, 'Simon Brady, blah, blah, blah,' it would have made more sense.

He went into the kitchen and prepared himself a breakfast, bread from the Italian bakery, with butter and jam, and more coffee. Munching in a desultory way, he thought that even this desire for breakfast was an indication that something in his life had gone seriously awry. When he was really working food ceased to matter; he drank coffee all day, and smoked, until dusk came and his stomach began to insist on food, and he realised that his fingers and hair were acrid with the smell of cigarettes. During their marriage Olivia would open a bottle of claret then, at twilight, which they would drink slowly while she made their meal. The wine would redden and darken in their glasses; she would move easily through the kitchen, feeding him olives, chunks of goat's cheese, raw mushrooms, to blunt his hunger while he waited. When things had begun to sour between them she had accused him of *making* her cook. *After all*, she had cried, arms akimbo, hair swinging, *I'm a painter, too.* But he hadn't made her cook; she had wanted to do it, had told him that it soothed her, had insisted on making the evening meals even after he'd become really famous and they could have dined every night in some chic SoHo bistro. But she had hated those restaurants, that cold glittering life, and she'd hated the girls. The girls had alarmed and dismayed her. Or perhaps she hadn't really been dismayed by the girls; perhaps she had been dismayed by his adolescent response to the girls.

He sighed, picturing Olivia, her stern equine beauty: lean face, level eyes, long wheat-coloured hair. Jesus, all he needed to make this day a real barrel of laughs was to conjure up the years with Olivia now! He was even thinking of going to Fanelli's again, despite the disaster with the German of a few months ago, when he remembered. That young woman, Claire Browne, was coming here this morning to be interviewed by him. Groaning inwardly, he thought, Please, God, let her not be a groupie; that would be too much.

# Chapter Four

Claire was glad she had decided to go on foot. She loved this time of day, when the East Village was sweet and still like an old European town. Avenue A was empty but for a few sturdy old men, walking doggedly, their pipe smoke dissolving in the watery light. They were probably on their way to one or another of the Russian coffee shops, to breakfast on eggs and sausages, read a Ukrainian newspaper, and talk amongst themselves with a kind of morose relish about the terrible state of this new world.

At night these streets sizzled with a hectic glamour. Artists sporting bohemian black, motorcycle boys, drug dealers, vagrants and suburban adolescents coursed indifferently past the Russian churches, which looked forlorn in their dignity, like decorous matrons who gather up their shawls and stare away into the distance. But in the morning the East Village still belonged to these old Russian men, and to the others who simply lived and worked here: fat Mrs Zakowski lumbering down First Avenue arm-in-arm with her shy middle-aged daughter; Mr Rugoff drawing back the grille from his cheese shop door; an Asian girl in paint-spattered jeans contemplating the window of Victor the Ravioli King.

It also belonged to someone Claire had come to know over the past year, a man whose strange life encompassed both the day and night-time worlds. Emory had lived in Tompkins Park before the mounted police descended there, one summer night not long ago, to rout the homeless. Claire remembered that night, the East Village hot and glossy with neon, restive as some exotic city, Singapore or Bangkok, kids on the corner of Ninth and A clustered round a radio and drinking beer, a party of transvestites hurrying down the avenue shrieking with laughter. Then the street suddenly darkening with policemen on horseback, and, before anyone could register what was happening, a skirl of hooves, a frantic glitter of metal, the flash of a baton as they poured into the park like Cossack hordes...

Now, banished from Tompkins Park, he slept in doorways and vestibules. She often saw him walking vaguely around in the morning, when he would engage her in curiously formal conversations about the weather, or about the novels he bought for a quarter from the hawkers along Saint Mark's Place, or about food (he would ask her for a few dollars so that he could have dumplings and tea at Vaselka's coffee shop). Today he was on Second Avenue, smoothing his hair, thick as putty with grime, back from his face, and dragging on a cigarette. He looked at her with his big bleached eyes and said, 'Hi, you look pretty.'

'Thanks. I'm going to a job interview.'

'Yeah? Cool. Good luck.' He finished his cigarette, ground it out under his broken boot; then immediately lit another. His hair was long and smoke-coloured; Claire thought that if it were washed it might be bright yellow. He had a sly oblique face, like a Sienese Madonna. He looked up. 'Man, I need a cup of coffee.'

She gave him a handful of coins from her bag. He said, 'Thanks. I think I'll go to the methadone clinic this afternoon. My social worker thinks I should go to the methadone clinic.'

'I didn't know you had a social worker, Emory.'

He gave her an embarrassed grin. 'Yeah, well.'

'Where is the clinic?'

'Chinatown, I think. But probably it's just bullshit. Probably it'll just be more bullshit.'

'But it might help you. Maybe you ought to give it a try.' He looked away. This was the most he'd ever revealed to her about his life. His eyes still averted, he asked, 'So how's your boyfriend?'

'Oh, you know I don't have a boyfriend.'

'Hey,' he said, looking at her again, with a smile, 'I'll be your boyfriend.'

'You are,' she answered, smiling back, 'You are my boy-friend.'

He laughed. This was easier ground, flirtation, the sexual banter of bars and other places he might have frequented in some former life. She said, 'I'd better go. I don't want to be late.'

'Have a nice job interview,' he called after her. He seemed to mean it.

She decided to walk west to Greenwich Village and then down towards SoHo. On MacDougal Street she noticed an Italian bakery window full of bread: long loaves bound with cord like firewood, gnarled *basti italiani*, *pane rotondi* with blistered crusts. Charmed, she walked in and saw, behind the counter and surrounded by more stalks and boulders of bread, a tall woman with a narrow head and a severe coiffure. This woman placed a hand on the collar of her black dress and smiled, and Claire couldn't stop staring at her; she had such a typically Mannerist face. In fact, she looked almost exactly like Germain Pilon's slender-headed bust of Mary Queen of Scots in the Louvre.

Claire bought a roll from the woman, to eat as she walked, laughing silently at herself. She knew that hers was a mad method of recognition, identifying that woman with Pilon's sculpture, or glancing in the street at a boy whose curls were bunched black and lustrous as grapes on his forehead and comparing him to a Caravaggio Bacchus, or likening her young Nigerian neighbour to the Charioteer at Delphi. After all, most people did not walk along the streets of New York deciding that some bus driver, or a weary lady trudging into the dry cleaners, resembled a Degas self-portrait or a Modigliani. But Claire had realised some time ago that her romantic perceptions enabled her to feel a bit more lustrous and unique, a bit less envious and ordinary, among the people whom she knew, encouraged her to believe that perhaps she was deserving of their favour, of admiration, or even love. And she had figured out as well that her fascination with art, her recognition of people in terms of paintings, served as a kind of protection against life, against uncertainty and pain. Anyway, she rationalised, it *is* lovely that such recognition is possible, that we carry, in our lineaments, the whole human story.

She herself had wide auburn eyes, unruly auburn hair, and an oval face. Her friend Zoë had once said that Claire's face convinced people she was very young and timid, but actually she was approaching thirty, with a doctorate in art history, and was not really timid at all. What she wanted was to write and publish and to travel, to leave New York and live abroad, perhaps in Ireland, or to sojourn on the Continent where she would walk through art galleries with painters and other art historians, and stop with them in cafés where working men would laugh softly, and their dark hands would lower biscuits into their glasses of wine.

Only sometimes Claire feared that she might resemble Madame Bovary, a character who could not bear the dull middle-classness of her life. Madame Bovary's spirit and body were desolate and yearned for *more*, but she could not conceive of it, this more that she desired, was certain only of its absence, which she experienced as crushing boredom. And so she took refuge in sentimental fantasies; she fed her longing for love on sticky bon-bons, and never came to understand the nature of what she wanted.

When Claire was a child, her mother had condemned her for lying, and Claire herself had believed she was a loathsome little liar; since now and again she would make up fanciful stories and was sometimes found out. So, she learnt to evade her loneliness and humiliation by spiriting herself into pictures, imagining that she was special, that she was different, that she was not really her horrible lying little self at all but *someone else*, that the real Claire lived in a quiet Flemish house where a cat slept on a chair in thick sunlight, or that she walked through woods in a long cream-coloured dress, carrying a picnic hamper. And she also tried to control her anger and disappointment through language, through using words like magical amulets. 'Sun-dappled,' she would murmur, walking to school in New York traffic, howling ambulances and screeching taxis, 'lambent, mellifluous.'

Now, walking up to Simon Brady's loft, she realised that she was trembling. For some reason she'd fastened her hopes on this interview, even though she had never pictured herself working at a job like this. Tedious, it would be, as her mother had said, and unconnected to her aspirations. Now, in a rare moment of real self-questioning, she suddenly asked herself, But do you *want* to abandon your ambitions, do you *want* to dream through your life, expecting someone to scoop you up in his palm and transport you to a better place? Is *that* what you want?

It was so hard to know what to feel, in this harsh and mercenary age, to distinguish real feeling from false, always trying not to seem foolish, *uncool*, the worst insult of all...

\* \* \*

The door was opened by a tall, slightly haggard, handsome man wearing jeans and a bulky green sweater. 'Come in,' he said, and then, indicating a red sofa, 'Would you like some coffee?' His words and gestures were curt, but he softened them with a small dry smile.

'Please don't trouble,' Claire said, 'unless you're making some.'

'I am.' He gave her an intent look; suddenly, his mouth curved up and his eyes narrowed in a deeper smile, and it was as though a finger brushed down her spine, a prickle of

38

something at once attractive and dangerous. 'I'll be just a minute,' he said briskly, and disappeared behind a partition into what she presumed was the kitchen.

She took off her jacket and walked over to the sofa. Why had he smiled at her in that dryly appraising, faintly sexual way? Had her demeanour struck him as inelegant, childish? Had he expected a taut, dark, scholarly-looking woman instead of herself, an unserious creature with masses of sherry-coloured hair, wearing a lavender dress bought for five dollars at some vintage clothing shop? Feeling slightly at a loss, she sighed, and looked about her.

The loft was cavernous as a cathedral; sunlight glossed its enormous window and settled in a great pool on the floor; in this light, motes seethed and spun, but everything else was still. An immense pink and blue painting, from Brady's colour-field abstraction days, completely covered one wall. She glimpsed, through an opening in another partition, a sun-washed work area: littered tables, canvases in a pile, brushes and palette knives.

He came out with two thick white cups, and while he handed her one she surreptitiously studied him. His features, she could see, had once been fine, but something, or things, had thickened them a bit. There were pouches under his eyes: a seasoned face. She supposed he was between forty-five and fifty.

He offered her a cigarette which she refused. 'Mind if I smoke?' he asked, smiling into her eyes. An intelligent smile, but the deliberate intensity of his gaze was still unnerving.

'No. Everyone around me smokes.'

'But you don't?'

'No,' she said again, and was immediately afraid he'd

think her prim. 'I have other vices,' she amended hastily, aware that his eyes, alert and blue, had still not stopped appraising her, and aware as well that her answer just now had been more suggestive than she had intended. Or what *had* she intended? All she knew was that this man's salt-blue eyes and rueful smile, even the way he drew on his cigarette, seemed to imply something intimate.

He laughed. 'Tell me your name again?'

'Claire Browne.'

He was still smiling softly. Well, two can stare, she said to herself, and let her gaze burn into his. He asked, 'Are you from New York, Claire Browne?'

'I was born here.'

'Peculiar, I wouldn't have thought so. You have no accent.'

'Sometimes I don't feel like a New Yorker.'

He tilted his head and regarded her even more closely. 'What *do* you feel like?'

Did he expect her to answer seriously, or flippantly? 'I don't know. An exile?'

He laughed again. 'Well, takes one to know one. I often don't know where I belong, either. And your parents. What are their backgrounds?'

'My father's family were mainly Irish Protestants, Huguenots who escaped persecution in France and settled in Cork. They made a lot of money when they came to America.' She affected solemnity. 'I am descended from merchant princes.'

'How unusual. I suppose they are not rich anymore, or you wouldn't be here applying for a job with me. And your mother's family?'

'Jews, from eastern Europe. My mother was born in the Bronx.'

'Any brothers or sisters?'

Startled, 'No.' What relevance had her next-of-kin to a minor job?

He was still giving her that gently sardonic smile. She thought she should be affronted by the boldness of his scrutiny, those blue eyes so unabashedly staring, and by all the personal questions he was so peremptorily firing at her, but she liked his bluntness, as though he had no patience for small talk. And of course she realised that his questions, and her answers, were an expression of this other thing which the two of them were feeling. She said, 'Where are *you* from, Mr Brady?'

'Please call me Simon. And if I may, I'd like to call you Claire.' He told her that he had been born in Gloucester, Massachusetts to first-generation Irish-Americans, and that his father, dead now, had been a doctor. His mother had been ailing all his young life, but her final sickness and then her death in his eleventh year had riven him. He had lived in New York since 1970, but had begun to have success as a painter only in 1978 or thereabouts. He'd had a wife once, but they were divorced five years ago. No children.

She hesitated; then asked, 'Are you interviewing anyone else for this job?'

'No. Darby Holland recommended you highly, and he's a man whose judgement I respect.' He narrowed his eyes against his own cigarette smoke. 'I presume you know what the job's about. I simply need an amanuensis.' They both smiled at the old-fashioned word. 'For quite a while I was considering engaging someone to help me organise my correspondence, only I never got around to it. But then, as you know, I was contacted by a woman who wants to do a biography.' He looked down briefly, as though uncomfortable alluding to his own fame. 'So I'd like to get my papers into some kind of order, which will be a formidable project, believe me. I'm not a well-organised person at all.' He paused. 'What I don't understand is why someone with your credentials – you have a doctorate in art history, don't you, and you write for *Art-Dimension*? – would want to take on a job like this. I don't expect that it will be intellectually stimulating.'

'But it will be a lot like what many art historians do.'

'You mean, art historians go through artists' papers and read their letters? Only those necrophiliacs do it to dead people, and you will have a *live* one to deal with.'

Claire looked into his eyes and saw the dry challenge there, and she knew that he knew she saw it. 'A live one,' she echoed.

He laughed again, softly. 'Something else. You know, I waffled about this project for about five months before I finally called you. I think I was afraid to unearth all my old cargo of letters and books and drawings, afraid of the emotions they might release, like opening Pandora's box – or boxes, in this instance. But Darby encouraged me to go through with it, and recently, so that I might understand how intelligent you are, he gave me one of your articles to read, on that Baroque picture by Moreno, the 'Saint Catherine'. You wrote about it so well, your rather romantic description of her hair, like a squall around her face.' He paused to light another cigarette. 'I enjoyed that piece. I've always liked good writing, which is rare for painters, I've been told, since we're supposed to be only visually minded. But I'm a close reader. And, also, Carlos Moreno has been on my mind these days.'

She waited for him to say more, but suddenly he got to his feet and gestured for her to follow. They walked over to his big colour-field painting. 'What do you think of this?' he asked in his abrupt way.

She examined the canvas. 'It reminds me a little of Monet, the Giverny series. But...'

He was smiling. 'Yes? Go on.'

She sensed that this was another challenge. 'Well, I don't know too much about Monet, but those Giverny paintings are so... I don't know, so beautiful. It's as though he were making this last voyage into light, into the heart of light. Such devotion, and *intelligence*...'

'I agree. Such intelligence, and care, while this painting–' he regarded it blandly '– this painting is just pigments sprayed from an aerosol canister onto a large canvas.'

Startled again, she asked, 'Did you like it when you painted it?'

'Yes. No. I thought it was pretty, but I suspected it wasn't good. I'd done better before, and I've done better since. I keep it here to help me maintain my sense of irony. Especially now, when fashion governs the art world. A few months ago this bombastic old German in a bar told me I was full of shit. Who knows? Maybe he was right.' He looked squarely at her, and extended his hand. 'Well, I am glad to meet you, Claire. Would you like to begin work on Monday?' Today was Thursday. 'We could try five hours per day, Monday through Friday, and see how that goes. Does nine till two seem sensible?' He laughed. 'I've never done anything like this before.'

Oh, yes you have, she thought. He went on, 'And the money? Is fifteen an hour all right for you?'

She wondered if he had expected her to ask for more. As if reading her mind, he said, 'If you need more, please tell me. We'll feel our way along.'

Again, she didn't know if it was something in her that made innuendo seem to resonate through almost everything he said, or if indeed he intended it so. His eyes told her he intended it. Swallowing, she said, 'Yes, I'll let you know.'

As she was leaving, he touched her cheek. 'I like your face. Maybe you will model for me?'

A simple request, or a classic invitation? Soon she would know, and decide what she wanted to do about it.

# Chapter Five

At the corner of Prince and West Broadway Claire glanced down and saw, spilling from a ruptured sack and powdering the gutter like moss, some yellow spice, saffron perhaps. It reminded her that the spice warehouses were just west, along the river; sometimes the wind in SoHo was redolent of cinnamon, coriander, cloves, coffee, as though New York were some exotic city with its wealth contained in bales of spices. The meat markets were also nearby – directly north of SoHo the world of trucks and bloodied cobblestones and scavenging gulls endured. And she remembered the egg warehouses, in TriBeCa. Her father had taken her there when she was a child, opening a heavy door onto tier upon tier of brown and cool white eggs glowing faintly in a vast dimness. She had seen how the eggs were candled for double yolks, which would bloom into life, floating magically within their fragile husks before the flame.

As she walked, she suddenly felt Simon Brady's hand on her face again. She was afraid her good judgement was faltering. She told herself that this man was probably just a pathological womaniser, but the suspicion seemed to do her no good; he was becoming, in her imagination, something else – and after just one brief meeting! But in England, once, she had seen a thirteenth-century painting of a girl walking through a cloister while reading a missal, and although she was meant to be pious she had struck Claire as erotic, somehow. Her head drooping like a flower over the little book, her yellow hair shawling her face: she had seemed to be moving in a dream of love. And Claire was remembering her now because it had occurred to her that she herself was yielding to a dream, some process of forgetting and transformation. Somehow Simon Brady had touched the green, secret heart of her desire, somehow his voice and eyes had kindled a heat in her that was melting the real man away – he was dissolving, to be replaced by the dream of him which he had ignited in her. He was talented and had flourished in the world, which were the things she desired for herself, and he had seemed to glimpse something attractive in her – a potent combination. She kept seeing his hard dry mouth, his heavy hands; dangerous, he was, but a danger she seemed to want.

You don't even know him, she admonished herself, but his intelligence, his warmth, had quickened something in her body and her weary heart just when she had begun to fear for them. Ah, it was true, she didn't know Simon Brady, but unless she was utterly mistaken this man with his deep looks and knowing smile had responded to her, also. And yes he was a dream, but surely something real could flower from a dream? Surely even love could begin with a dream of love?

Sighing, she strolled along, feeling a bit as though it were her first day in a foreign country, when ordinary things are lovely with strangeness. Well, she did approach life too romantically, as her old boyfriend Jeremy had often told her. For instance, Emory, her drug addict acquaintance: it was fine for her to think that his dirty hair looked like tarnished gold, but what did she know of his real life, of what it was like to go filthy and wretched for days needing only that one killing thing? Jeremy had ceaselessly chastened her for romanticising the East Village, its daytime world of Russian immigrants drinking borscht in the coffee shops ('Are you serious, Claire? Do you really think that the lives of old, impoverished, anti-Semitic refugees are sweet and magical?') and its night world of clubs and gallery openings ('Do you really believe that all those mediocre painters, dissolute hangers-on, and nar-cissistic fashion designers are brave and defiant, instead of just fatuous? What's wrong with you?') Maybe what was wrong with her had something to do with her mother's coarseness. Cecily was the kind of working-class New York woman who bellowed at taxi drivers and terrorised people in shops if she suspected they were overcharging her, a nasty, stevedore-like form of behaviour which had always embarrassed her daughter.

Stopping at the Korean market to buy vegetables for dinner, Claire wondered if her cynical pal Zoë would have liked Simon Brady. She knew a few women who'd have suspected him the moment he opened his suave mouth, but not I, she thought, not I. She had liked him because he was gifted and accomplished, and also because he'd seemed bright, sexy, and even kind, but now she thought perhaps he really was just a callous old goat and the reason she didn't care was that she expected too little of love. She remembered an animal she'd seen at the Bronx Zoo, some nocturnal creature; it had looked so small and hungry in the artificial darkness of its home, willing to feed on dust; it had stared at her with its immense eyes like lamps, a kindred spirit.

\* \* \*

Zoë's rough slow voice said, 'If I had a nickel for every time I fucked some boy in a taxi, I would be a rich woman.' Her right hand caressed her bare left arm. She had drawn her hair into a chignon today; its darkness and profusion reminded Claire of the Edwardian portraits in her grandmother Fabienne's dining room, of women whose heads were tilted back as though pulled by the weight of their gathered-up hair. 'One true thing about my life,' Zoë continued, delicately removing a piece of tobacco from her tongue, 'It has made me a specialist on the colour of pricks.' She began, coolly, to enumerate on her fingers: 'There are the big red ones like church bulbs, the sweet pink ones, the angry purple ones, the yellow vegetable ones, the black police batons, the pale Irish uncircumcised ones with their little nun's wimple.' She paused to light another cigarette, and for a moment its smoke was suspended between them, a grey tissue on the bright air. 'All the colours of the rainbow, honey.'

Claire asked, 'Have you ever been in love, Zoë?'

She laughed softly. 'I never told you about Beauregard? He was the passion of my life. He had those eyes that bulge out a little, but he was handsome nevertheless. He was a black man from down South, a musician. Tenor saxophone. Jesus, it would make me cry; he was so fine on that thing.'

'What happened to him?'

Zoë inclined her head so that her long silver earring touched her shoulder. 'He died. People said it was drugs, but they always say that about musicians. People also used to say that he was mean, because he didn't talk much, but Beau was a lamb, and the reason he didn't talk was because he was listening. Once he told me that at night, every night, the stars actually sing, a kind of silver music in the sky. "Hush," he would say, "Just listen." That is why he died, I think, that is why. He heard those stars singing.'

'Oh, my dear.' They were silent a moment. It was the day after Claire's interview, and Zoë had phoned to ask her round for coffee, after which they were to go out to lunch. The afternoon was hot for spring; sunlight fumed in through Zoë's dirty window, warming the coffee table on which her black cat lolled beside a white dish heaped with cigarettes, a copy of *Vogue* magazine, a blue powder compact, two decaying peaches, a pot of rouge.

Although Zoë had been born of sedate parents in New Iberia, Louisiana, she had embraced a darker life long ago. At fifteen, while her friends were gossiping dreamily about boys and reading magazines that counselled them on make-up and romance, Zoë, naked under her overcoat, had walked along the local highways, among cars frozen in heavy traffic, offering blow-jobs to the bored businessmen for ten bucks. Now, thanks to her exclusive clientele, her life was much less dangerous, as well as fairly prosperous, but despite her beauty she often looked dissipated to Claire, who had begun noticing pouches under her friend's narrow, topaz-coloured eyes, and something blurred and bruised about her mouth. She'd met Zoë at a gallery launching just over a year ago, and had been both shocked and intrigued by the life this young woman had seemed to live, her dining table cluttered with spilled face powder, glasses of cognac, plates of ossifying cheese and sweaty sausages on which she ground out her cigarettes, lamps at either end made of dolls wearing pink organza dresses, under which light bulbs burned. And Zoë herself had shocked and intrigued her, mad Zoë with her dirty kitten's face, her languorous body, her tough, funny, intelligent mind, her alarming work. Claire, wondering why she would befriend such a woman, had concluded that Zoë's dark life must have called out to the disappointed places in her own heart; that Zoë's wildness must have appealed to her own suppressed passions. Anyway, friendships with lowlife types were commonplace enough in bohemian New York.

Now Claire asked, 'What did Beauregard think of your job?'

'Oh, baby, he didn't like it. He wanted me to stop, but I said no. I said, "I *like* my double life." She paused. 'What do *you* think of my job?'

'Why, Zoë, you are a goddess, a love goddess.'

Zoë threw back her head and gave a roar of laughter. '*Cherie*, you are too *much*.' Again they were quiet, gazing at the slumbering cat, the dust-furred coffee table. Presently Zoë touched Claire's shoulder and said, 'Listen, how did your interview go? Did you get the job? How much money?'

'Fifteen an hour,' answered Claire, a bit sheepishly, 'Half days, five days a week.'

'Jesus!' Zoë gave a derisive snort, 'A pretty girl like you. I could get you work tonight that would make you three hundred dollars before tomorrow morning.'

Choosing to ignore this, Claire said, 'I'm okay financially. My *ArtDimension* articles bring in a bit of steady money, and I'm trying to be frugal with the small savings I inherited from my grandmother. So I'm doing okay, for now, but I do feel anxious. I mean, I couldn't possibly ask my parents for help, if anything were to go wrong. First of all, they haven't very much money any more, and second, I wouldn't want to appeal to my mother in that way, especially not these days. No, I realise I must change my life, write my book. And I will, I will. Only I can't seem to get started, I don't know why...'

Zoë crushed out her cigarette. 'Anyway, we should celebrate your new job. Want to go to a party? That SoHo painter, Ted Rubenstein, invited me to a *soirée* at his loft tonight. He is a friend of mine, not a client or anything, and people say his parties are *très* cool. Might be fun?'

'Might be,' echoed Claire doubtfully, picturing throngs of ultra-*chic* SoHoites slouching around some vast loft. She usually preferred East Village parties, but, then again, maybe Simon Brady would be there. 'Thanks, Zoë,' she said, 'I'd like to go.'

\* \* \*

When they walked up to Rubenstein's loft, what they saw looked like a Cinecittà Roman orgy. The odours of booze, good perfume on unwholesome skin, and marijuana smoke curdled the air; abandoned wine glasses crowded all the tables, and the floor was muddied with big puddles of beer in which paper plates, napkins, and trodden-on pieces of cheese were drowning. The entire place was dark, smouldering and impossibly full of people: a golden-haired girl in a golden dress dancing by herself, her arms out, head thrown back, her face rosy and laughing; two men, both with sorrowful Byzantine faces, smoking pot and caressing each other's slender hands; a film star dancing clumsily and laughing at his awkwardness; an old woman wearing a purple ballgown encrusted with jewels. A man had wrenched open a woman's silver blouse and was kissing her naked breasts; her long hair had tumbled clammily down over her arms; she stared without expression at his head while she suckled him. Claire recognised her colleague Brian Solonik smiling at a man wearing dreadlocks and round Karl Marx glasses. Zoë screamed in her ear, 'Hey, let's get some of that champagne.'

Chapter Five

* * *

Claire soon lost Zoë in the crowd, but she didn't mind. She wandered around, drinking from her sweaty glass of champagne and looking at the people. Suddenly, a lupine man came up and asked her, in an English accent, to dance. He danced with his lean head tilted back, his eyes narrowed and his mouth thinly smiling, as though she amused him but not all that much. Afterwards, he touched her elbow and said, 'Let me bring you some wine. Are you a painter like Ted?'

'No. I write about paintings.'

Behind them, a woman whose lips and cheeks were rouged the colour of dried blood and a man dressed all in white were dipping two tiny spoons into a vial of cocaine.

The eyes of Claire's dancing partner glittered like icicles. 'Good God, a critic.'

'No. I write about dead people's paintings.'

He smiled with relief. 'An art historian. My old girlfriend was an art historian. I adored her, but she left me, and not, I must tell you, because I was an impoverished sculptor, but because I am Catholic. She loathes Catholicism.'

Claire said, 'I like Catholicism because it's so ancient. I like cassocks and those orchards of candlelight you see in the churches, and I like the Latin. Are you an intellectual Catholic like Graham Greene?'

'Yes, indeed. I'm a convert like him as well. I was born a nice English Protestant, and I am still an English gentleman, which is why I brought you that nice glass of wine you are drinking. Are you Catholic, then?'

She shook her head no. 'Why did you convert?'

'Ah,' he answered, looking at her with his lead-coloured eyes, 'To tell you *that* story, I should have to come visit you with a bottle of champagne and a gram of cocaine, and then we'd have a long talk.'

She noticed, behind him, a woman whose dress was made of some black shiny stuff; when she moved, blue and red lights darted from it so that it looked to Claire like the shimmering hide of some mythical creature, a dragon or a griffin. The woman's skin was very white, and she was smiling up at a splendidly handsome black man whose hands were gliding slowly over her bare arms. Suddenly, a chill glinted down Claire's back. She was appalled to realise that she was feeling slightly attracted to her own, snide dancing partner, maybe, perversely, because she didn't like him. Looking at his thin mouth, she thought, It's on that glib tongue the priest places the wafer, and I...

'...like Simon Brady,' he was saying.

'What?'

He gave his wolfish smile. 'I know his former wife; she's English, you see. Poor Olivia, she was absolutely *eclipsed* by him, couldn't paint at all. It happens so often, don't you agree? Clever women attach themselves to these famous artists and are *consumed*.'

'Do you know Brady also, or only his ex-wife?'

'I know him glancingly, and not through Olivia. I met him about a year ago, at a party in London. He was talking *ad infinitum* about Art and Meaning and so forth. Quite tiresome, I thought, since he'd done nothing new or interesting in about eight years.' He laughed. 'You must think I am being spiteful, but I feel no jealousy towards Brady. In fact I am *never* jealous; it's too exhausting, and besides, envy is one of the seven deadly sins.' He touched her arm again. 'And even if I did resent Brady's immoderate success, I'd be a fool to discuss it here, where he might walk in at any moment.'

'Oh!' said Claire, who had given up on this possibility, 'Is he expected here, tonight?'

The Englishman looked quizzically at her. 'I presume so. They tell me that Rubenstein's gatherings have become quite the thing, lately. So you know Brady?'

'No, not really,' she answered hurriedly, and backed away into the crowd.

\* \* \*

She walked into the kitchen and saw Brian Solonik again, lounging drunkenly on a blue settee, his left arm thrown around the shoulders of a thin girl who looked stoned, and his right embracing an older, grey-haired woman who was talking into his ear. He gave Claire a vague smile. Sighing, she went into another room and looked out of its broad window at the old iron buildings dreaming in the moonlight. As she pressed her forehead, which felt hot, against the cool glass, she felt someone come up next to her. The voice asked, 'What are you looking at?'

'The street,' she answered, 'The empty street, and the

sheen on those buildings over there.'

'Why are they shining, do you think?'

'They are shining,' she said, still not looking at him, 'from within.'

He laughed. 'Probably it's only because they are made of iron, but I much prefer your theory. I too believe they are shining from within.'

She withdrew her attention from the window, and smiled at him, his fine blue eyes and rueful face making her feel suddenly intensely shy. 'Hello, Simon.' Also smiling, he answered, 'What a surprise! I must say, I am glad to see you here. Are you having a good time?'

'Not bad, considering the crush and the noise. It's strange, I don't know Ted Rubenstein; I don't even know what he looks like.'

'I'm afraid you're not missing much. Ted is a horse's ass, and to be honest I only come to his silly parties for the booze, which is usually pretty good.' He seemed to hesitate. 'Why don't we leave this place and go for a walk along Prince Street?'

She felt herself blush with pleasure, but something made her pause, and it wasn't just a reluctance to leave Zoë in the lurch. It was more that she didn't want to hasten things; very soon she would be venturing into this man's home, and indeed into his life, reading his personal letters, plunging into his papers. Soon enough something would happen, but now she would not hurry. 'I'd love to,' she replied, 'But I am here with my friend.'

'I see,' he said, rather dryly, and she immediately realised that he had misunderstood. 'Is your friend Brian

Solonik?' he asked brusquely, 'Someone mentioned he was here tonight.'

'Oh, no,' she assured him, 'I do know Brian, we work together at *ArtDimension* of course, but my friend is a woman, a fascinating Creole called Zoë.'

'I see,' he repeated, but more easily this time. He paused to light a cigarette. 'Speaking of *ArtDimension*, remember I told you that your article on Carlos Moreno's "Saint Catherine" was especially interesting to me? Well, just last week my friend Owen Kettlethorpe informed me that he's been studying a painting in Paris which he thinks might be a Moreno. It was gathering dust in some apartment and nobody knew.'

Owen Kettlethorpe was the world's foremost authority on Baroque painting. Claire took a deep breath. 'Really? My God, how exciting...'

'You mustn't tell anyone. After reading your piece I knew the news would please you, so I'm letting you in on it even though I promised Owen I'd keep it on the QT. He's nervous as hell that the information will trickle out and create wild rumours. Of course, I haven't seen the painting, I don't even know the subject, but if it really is an Old Master...'

'I know, I know,' she murmured, staring at him. She was thinking that her distress about her father had so dulled her, she had nearly forgotten her joy in work, that thrumming in the blood, a literal watering of the mouth – and if this painting were genuine it would be such a marvellous discovery: a lost canvas by the Spanish Baroque master, Carlos Moreno! She had loved writing about his 'Saint Catherine', whose large dark eyes, round white arms, and disordered hair were warmed with such a disturbing sexiness. To many puzzled scholars, this shining creature had seemed utterly unlike the pious maiden of legend, nor had Moreno depicted her with any of Saint Catherine's usual emblems: the Catherine wheel, or books in homage to her wisdom. Claire's article had asked, Could Carlos Moreno really have wanted to portray a *saint* in this way, as an earthy young woman, her eyes and cheeks glowing with such a human ardour? And the answer she had proposed was a firm yes, because Moreno, like his pal Caravaggio, had been influenced by humanism, and the Saint Catherine of his imagination might very well have been just such a girl, a human girl, with black hair and a strong white throat and a passionate demeanour. And now, another Moreno, as yet unknown to the world! Claire wanted to ask more, but paused, aware that she must temper her excitement, since this knowledge was a subtle gift from Simon to herself. 'You mustn't tell anyone,' Simon repeated, smiling in his wry way, 'But I will keep you informed.'

He tilted towards her, and Claire thought that he might kiss her; she had a sensation of falling down through the dark air; he had come so close that she could smell the cigarette smoke on his breath, but then a deep male voice cried, 'Simon, where the hell have you been?'

A plumpish florid man, his right hand clutching an unopened bottle of red wine, his left encircling the skinny arm of a dark-haired girl, was grinning lopsidedly. 'Jesus Christ, Simon! All night I've been wanting to introduce you to Gwendolyn here. Great kid, Gwendolyn.' The girl closed her eyes slowly, like a disdainful cat. Oblivious, the man went on, 'I was looking all over this fucking loft for you. I hadn't realised I'd invited all these fucking has-beens and nobodies tonight. Or maybe none of 'em were invited. Maybe my home has been invaded by tourists and strangers!' He laughed raucously. He was ignoring Claire, but she realised that the girl's eyes, elongated with black make-up, were staring at her. With curiosity? Malevolence? Appraising her hairstyle? She didn't care, and, anyway, she'd had enough. Slowly she eased away and dipped back into the next room.

* * *

It was nearly dawn. Claire waited at the bathroom door till two girls, both tall and lovely as models, emerged staggering and giggling into each other's shoulders. What had they been doing in there? Drugs, or sex, or both? She went in and splashed cold water on her face.

Looking for Zoë, she saw the rotund man and drowsy-eyed girl again, slouching against the window and drinking wine in gulps from their bottle, but it seemed that Simon had gone. Lucky him, Claire thought. But presently she saw him, looking down at Brian Solonik who was still sprawled on the blue sofa, although his companions had abandoned him. Suddenly (and surprisingly, considering his evident torpor), Brian jumped to his feet and began to stagger towards Simon with clenched fists. 'Fuck you!' he cried. Typical, thought Claire, through her astonishment. While he could be witty in print, Brian was often loutishly inarticulate in person. A sullen fellow, he had a reputation for pugnacity, but Claire had never seen him turn physically violent until this moment. 'You're a shit, Brady,' he shouted – again with dazzling originality – and tried to punch Simon in the face, but Simon seized his wrists and said evenly, 'I'm not going to brawl with you, Solonik, you talentless weasel. Here's a suggestion: instead of writing your pathetic articles, why don't you just go and fuck your pal Luke Reilly up the ass?' He whirled round and stalked out of the kitchen. Thinking confusedly that since she worked with Brian she should apologise for his behaviour, Claire began, hesitantly, to follow Simon, but before she could call out to him he had left, banging the door behind him.

She jumped when Brian touched her shoulder. 'You heard that?' he asked, frowning perplexedly. She saw that he was very drunk: his dark-blond hair had spilled into his bleary eyes, and he was listing to the right. 'You heard that, Claire? Why did he say that, about me fucking Luke Reilly up the ass? Why did he say that? I'm not gay.' His frown deepened. 'Or am I?'

'Never mind, Brian.' She took his arm. 'Come back to your sofa and have a snooze.'

'All right,' he mumbled grumpily. She lowered him back onto the settee; then went out to continue looking for Zoë, whom she finally located standing at the window next to the plump, wine-guzzling man and his skinny Gwendolyn. 'Hi, baby,' called Zoë. 'Have you met Ted yet?'

The plump man gave her a shrewd look. Was it because she had been talking intently with Simon before, or because he was wondering if she might be one of Zoë's colleagues? Anyway, his small eyes, hard and bright as polished pebbles, made her uncomfortable. And the girl Gwendolyn was once again staring at her in a heavy, insolent way. 'Yes,' said Claire resignedly, 'We've met, I suppose. At least, we were side by side in the same space.'

All of a sudden, in a far corner of the enormous room, a woman began to scream at a tall blond man, 'Betrayed me! Betrayed me!' Her face was mottled with anguish or rage, and her curly orange hair seemed to crackle around her head. The man's hands were extended; he was trying to soothe her but she would have none of it, and, as the loft became abruptly quiet, listening, she proceeded to take off her clothes. Still screaming, she tugged off her purple dress and threw it at him; underneath, she had on a black bra and black stockings; these came off, too. When the woman was naked, the wan morning light, granular as talc, blanched her thin body with its pronounced ribs and its orange hair like a spurt of fire between her legs. 'Bastard!' she screamed, 'Liar!' and then again, 'Betrayed me, betrayed me!' She began to sob; the man tried to take her in his arms but she howled, her head thrown back, her face contorted in a rigor of grief, like Rodin's 'Head of Sorrow'.

The stereo was still on and now Ella Fitzgerald's voice cascaded into the room; everyone was frozen, staring at the woman, except for the movie star, slumped in a corner with his head in his arms, ill or unconscious.

Suddenly, a young man appeared with an overcoat; he threw it over the girl's body like someone capturing butterflies. She collapsed in his arms. 'Come,' he crooned, 'C'mon, my dear, let's go.' Zoë touched Claire's arm. 'Yeah, honey, let's go.'

# Chapter Six

They stopped for breakfast at a twenty-four-hour coffee shop. It was empty except for a scrawny girl with purple hair eating bacon and eggs, and an old man whose lean, bearded face made him look like Michelangelo's Moses. The waiters, all Greek boys with sensuous eyes and pink cheeks, were lounging behind the counter drinking coffee from I LOVE NEW YORK paper cups, and laughing softly, probably at the absurdity of life in this twenty-four-hour town, full of grizzled Old Testament figures and punk girls with bizarre hair eating breakfast at ungodly hours.

Claire said, 'That woman, the one who took off her clothes. How had the man betrayed her, do you think?'

Zoë stopped buttering her bagel long enough to give Claire a deeply exasperated look. 'Honey, I declare, sometimes I despair of you. How do you *think* he betrayed her? You are nearly thirty years old and you have lived your whole life in New York City. At least I used to be an old-fashioned convent schoolgirl in Louisiana, so if I went around with big eyes asking questions like that, I would have *some* excuse, but you do not have one single excuse in the whole world, Claire Browne, except that you do not want to face life. And that is one pitiful excuse, because life is not *so* terrible. You do not *have* to live in a storybook, child, you can live in the world.' Her voice softened. 'And *you* are not so terrible, either. You do not have to be so innocent and good the whole damn time because underneath you are afraid that you might really be hungry and desperate. *Everybody* is hungry and desperate, and vicious, too, sometimes.'

Claire accepted this; she was not without the power of self-scrutiny. It was just that those of self-deception were greater and more subtle. Now she thought of her old boyfriend Jeremy. Why had she ever involved herself with such an unkind and abrasive man in the first place? The answer came to her promptly: because she'd been terribly lonely. Of course she knew that the prospect of living alone in vibrant New York was exhilarating to many young women, yet she herself had had little joy in it. Alone in her apartment, a panel of sunlight sloping in through the window onto the quiet table, the art books, the painterly bowl of fruit; the staccato cries of children in Spanish and English floating up from Avenue A; at twilight trying to open her door while juggling a clutch of late bills, a carton of milk, some vegetables and cheese, and then listening to the answering machine... She'd had her pleasure in work, but it had been dry and brief. It had been as though there were no pith, no richness of hue or texture, in her life.

# Chapter Six

She'd had her own centre, from which the work had flowed, but where was the sweet friend with whom she could talk about the work, about her day, about her fears? And when her father was diagnosed with Alzheimer's a weight had fallen on her shoulders so easily she scarcely knew she was carrying it, but she began to move in a leaden, deliberate way through her days, and when she came home there was still no-one, no kind lips or arms to comfort her. And this lack of sweetness was so great that she could not let herself know she was feeling it; after all, it would have been the measure of her need, would have sounded the depths of a pain so appalling she would not, could not, believe it existed.

Her disappointments as a child had made her hungry for love, and yet, precisely because she was so disappointed, she could not fully believe that this hunger might be assuaged. And so she had settled for less. She had settled her need for love (and the need itself had seemed to her shameful) on objects who by their very nature could not fulfil it. She had settled for the meagre or the false because she'd been terrified of having nothing at all; she'd settled for the unsteady, the capricious, because she'd thought that they were all she deserved; she had convinced herself that she loved men who were shallow, feckless, untender. And at times she had even exploited men as vulnerable as herself, carried away by her own murmured blandishments, because these men had served to ease her loneliness for a time, and because she had understood, cravenly, that they would not leave her.

Or she had adored and idealised certain unlikely men whom for some reason she had believed might rescue her, and that was where Jeremy had come in. She'd known what he was – arrogant, self-regarding, expecting homage as his due.

And yet she hadn't known, had chosen not to know. A moderately talented, moderately successful young novelist, he had impressed her with his intelligence and his exotic past so curiously like her own. He was a hybrid too, the only child of a spoilt upper class English mother and a renegade film director-gambler, Jewish-American father. She had thought she understood him; she had looked at him, his handsome, sometimes cold, sometimes hurt face, and she had felt an answer in her own body, Ah, I know you.

But she had known only her own desire for love; the man himself had not come into focus for a long time. At first she had been both thrilled and repelled by his cynicism. He had seemed to her deep and sophisticated, with his heavy drinking and roguish past. But Jeremy's cynicism had not been a glamorous attitude, an unwillingness to suffer fools gladly: no, she had learnt soon enough that it was harsh, and real, some old wound had indeed soured his spirit. As he became more and more defeatist his books, once astringent and wry, deteriorated into ugly tirades, and the drinking did not ease, as she'd thought it might, but worsened, and grew, for her, into a source of real pain. She hadn't known if he was seeing other women, and was glad she didn't know, since her fragility in that area was so considerable.

Their final break, after five years of living together, had come while they were on a holiday in the south of Spain. She remembered the day: they had stopped for drinks at a café called Ricardo's. She'd loved its sudden dimness after the bright road, and the men slouching at the bar, their voices heavy in the air. Looking out the open door she had seen, as in a triptych, one vine spilling over a green shutter, a bicycle sprawled against an ochre wall, and two dogs sleeping on the pavement

– never had she seen such things, or smelled this smell (a distillation of earth, hot stone, coffee, and olive oil), in America.

Then they went back to their hotel room, which was fiercely hot; she took off her clothes and lay on the clean bed; one drop of sweat trickled between her breasts. It was siesta-time and silent except for a sudden laugh from the plaza like a spatter of rain against their window, and the abrupt roar of a motorcycle. When Jeremy closed the shutters a pencil of light flashed in their seam; he came over to the bed and looked down at her. The foreignness of this place, its heat and indolence, were firing her with a kind of sad lust, sad because on this journey she had finally let herself know that she did not love him, and also because she could see by the look in his eye that he was going to hurt her, humiliate her, and she would like it.

Still on his feet, he extended his hand and touched her left nipple, which immediately stiffened for him. He caressed her stomach; then slowly settled his hand on her inner thigh. Desire was making her throat thick, but she remained still. 'Answer me,' he said softly, 'I want you to tell me...' Under his languorous hand her skin was growing moist with sweat and excitement. He repeated, 'Tell me...'

'*What?*' she whispered. Their room was concealed from the dusty plaza; anybody looking up would see only the closed green eye of their window. Soon the strident sunlight would deepen to honey, and then people would emerge from their apartments and stroll out to the bars, to drink sherry poured from black casks, and eat plates of cool ham, strong sheep's cheese, prawns, artichoke hearts dripping oil. And she and Jeremy would be among them, in a bar where hams hung from the ceiling like chandeliers, a loving holiday couple eating tapas, drinking wine.

Jeremy murmured, 'Your hair is such a dark red, like amber, or like the dark sherry they drink here. And your eyes are the same colour as your hair. But this is a chestnut colour.' He touched her pubic hair. 'My dear, you are covered in dew.'

'Jeremy,' she said harshly, 'please stop talking like the seducer in a stupid play.'

He laughed. 'But it's true, you are lovely, and I do love you.' Still fully dressed, he lay down beside her, and, taking her in his arms, kissed her temples, her lips, her damp throat. Oh, Jeremy, she thought, About as much as I love you.

He was being deliberately slow, tormenting her. This dark and miserable lust was boiling in her and she thought, Listen to him, listen to him using ridiculous rococo diction and affected endearments, and though he were some swashbuckling ladykiller, Beau Brummel or a Hogarth rake or Casanova. Again he commanded, 'Claire, tell me...'

'What? Tell you *what?*' He began, finally, to caress her more intimately. She shuddered. 'Tell me,' he whispered, 'What would you like me to do to you?'

'I would like you to make love to me, please,' she said evenly.

He kissed her. 'How much do you want it?'

'Oh, I hate you.'

'That's good. It's better when you hate me.'

She looked up into his remote face. A weak bloom of sunlight the shutters hadn't kept out struck his left cheek; his eyes were glistening. 'Do you care about me at all?' she whispered.

'Do you care about *me?*' His hand stroked and stroked her. She closed her eyes and said softly, 'You monster, if it were only possible I would have loved to love you.'

'You do love me, darling. You love me this much.' She

groaned. She was all drenched and aching; the coverlet ground into her back. She began thinking about incidental things. She thought that this room smelled indefinably of southern Europe, of sun-soaked stone, of heavy beds in shuttered hotels. She thought about Jeremy in a restaurant the night before, his hand, the hand that was making love to her now, dipping a petal of artichoke into oil...

Oh, but this was sweet; he was kissing the whorls of her ear. His old girlfriend Molly had said, 'Be careful', but Claire had wanted him, had believed, foolishly, vainly, that she could soothe him, balm his wounds, and he hers. She should have known; he was a drunk like her mother: was that why she was drawn to him? Had she believed that if only she were penitent enough, good enough, the very source of pain could become one of comfort? That, if only she tried hard enough, all the betrayals she had ever known could be converted into blessings? How often had she kissed him, salting her lips with his self-reproachful tears, while he apologised for reviling her the night before when he had come home too maddened with booze and bitterness to even know who she was? People called her idealistic but she knew at that moment in the Spanish hotel that she was a cynic, that she moved through an arid country, looking for love in the place of sorrow, believing that there was nothing else, only this ancient grief and fear, only promises broken on the dry ground, only appeasement for a time, before the blow fell again. And why did she continue to look for love in such a barren place? Probably because she was not brave enough to leave it, because she was convinced that any other place must be only a mirage...

She opened her eyes now and stared into her boyfriend's unloved face. Jeremy, she thought, I have to get away from you. He was smiling, he was excited, scandalous when they were supposed to be chastely asleep in the separate rooms the hotel had booked for them because they had different surnames. The concierge had disapproved, she'd seen his professional smile dissolve and his mouth close stiffly when Jeremy had given him a level look: 'One double bed please.' She brought her fingers up to his lower lip which was lovely and full. He had taken off his clothes and now he was pressing his dry hot body against hers, she lifted her pelvis and he plunged easily into her; his mouth against her ear murmured filthy exciting words and she clutched his back, closed her eyes again, and screamed, but on her own, always on her own.

A week later, back in New York, she moved out.

\* \* \*

Now Zoë said, 'Honey, what are you thinking about?'

She was thinking that maybe she was swirling, spiralling, down into some vortex with Simon Brady. Maybe he was just another Jeremy, and she, obdurate and gullible, would succumb – predictably, boringly – again. Maybe, like the fish caught again and again, water falling away in sheets from its body, she simply would not learn. She was deliberately stupid, she would never let experience season her, but she would walk in to trouble anyway, fey, disingenuous, deceiving herself and perhaps others, merely because other people's lives had always seemed to her more exciting than her life, her house. Cecily a stone angel beating her breast, her father asleep in his armchair before the blue TV...

# Chapter Seven

Saturday morning at eleven, Simon's intercom shrilled. When he answered, a nasal girl's voice said, 'Hi. It's Gwendolyn. Don't you remember me?'

His weary memory pitched, rummaged, faltered; finally, an image of Ted Rubenstein's sullen, undernourished girlfriend of the night before materialised. Her insistent voice continued, 'Hey, won't you let me in?'

'All right, but not for long. I'm working.' This was a lie; reluctant to attempt work, he had been eating a disgusting but satisfying breakfast of cold ravioli and sodden salad, and reading the paper. But he resented this creature appearing, encroaching on his day as if it were her right. On the other hand he couldn't bring himself bluntly to spurn her.

Only after he'd consented to let her up did it occur to him, disturbingly, that he had seen her before last night.

\* \* \*

'Can I have a cigarette?' She sidled into the room, hands deep in the pockets of her jeans. She had a lissom body, and a sharp face with small, heavily painted eyes. Her smile was sly and presumptuous.

'Listen, young woman, why don't you just tell me why you are here? I haven't all the time in the world.'

Hands still in her pockets, she lowered herself onto the arm of the sofa. Her insolence, a kind of serene audacity, was unnerving him. She seemed way too cool, too confident for her years. And he was still troubled by the vague feeling that he'd seen her somewhere before.

She was still smiling; saying nothing, sphinx-like with those kohl-blackened eyes. He gave her a cigarette and ventured, 'How's my pal Ted?'

She said in a low voice, 'You're such a shit, Simon. It was only five years ago, you son of a bitch.'

'Five years?' He was too startled to be chagrined at not remembering this feral little creature, with whom, apparently, he'd had some sort of tryst – her manner was too blatantly sexual for it to have been anything else. But she really did look no older than nineteen or twenty. 'Five years? You must have been only a child!'

She blew smoke towards him. 'I'm older than I look. I was a student then, at Pratt. You came to give a boring talk and then there was a party. And then you brought me home with you. You brought me *here*.' She waved her arms to encompass the whole loft.

Simon stared at her. It was true that after the collapse of his marriage he had indulged in a prolonged period of promiscuity, which had been fairly easy, because he'd been a new, fashionable painter, and the girls (aspiring artists, eager models, students, socialites) had seemed almost literally to tumble in and out of his life – and his bed. They had served a number of purposes, those girls. His marriage had actually withered years before the divorce, but the final, formal break with Olivia had thrown him off balance, as had his new fame. While the success and money were certainly splendid, he'd panicked because the changes in his life were so great. Everything that had been sure, all his moorings – his home, Olivia, the rhythm of their days, their friends – all this had been disrupted. He would open his eyes at three or four in the morning rigid with an ancient fear, the same terror that he had sometimes felt as a boy at night, after his mother's death, when the world beyond his window had seemed perilous, bereft of love, and he had placed a hand over his heart to make sure it was still beating.

So the girls had distracted him. He hadn't loved them, not one, had not wanted to after the exhausting Olivia years. But they had been determined, bright, ardent, and he had arrogantly considered them his due, the fruits of his fame. He had stopped only when he'd come to the conclusion that profligacy was a real danger. It hadn't had anything to do with morality; it had to do with a dulling of the spirit: the pleasures were so easy he soon realised that he had almost ceased to feel them. And the girls, although amusing and pleasant, could not soothe his sore mind and heart, or even his body, for very long, nor could he satisfy them except on the shallowest level – he barely knew them, after all.

But before he had come to this conclusion his increasing loneliness, and a growing self-disgust, had combined to make him a bit frenzied. He was having more and more affairs, with girls who were less and less interesting to him except on a primitively physical level. And he was even getting muddled, so that there were times he bustled some woman out of his loft, practically throwing her clothes at her and pushing her out the door, before some other candidate arrived.

Now, in this context, he finally remembered Gwendolyn. It had been one of the most trifling encounters of his chequered career, but he supposed he ought to feel grateful to her now, because his embarrassment after their two nights together had helped him to determine to change his ways.

Tired and slightly drunk after his talk at Pratt, which had been followed by the obligatory wine and cheese and stilted conversation, he'd been eager to get back home as fast as possible. But as he was climbing into the taxi a skinny girl with glossy black hair had hurried out of the college crying, 'Hey, take me with you?'

It had been a night of less than bliss. He had thought he might be too weary to exert himself for her, but something about her, a snideness, an effrontery, something in her mean eyes taunted him, igniting in him an angry lust. And when she began to ridicule him, to tell him he was an old man, couldn't get it up properly, was convinced he was a genius just because some rich collectors had bought his miserable paintings, he was so inflamed with rage that he had fucked her violently all night.

A week or so later she was at some party at the Guggenheim, and he, remembering the distasteful but thrilling combination of fury and lust which she had inspired in him, was drawn to her again, despite himself. This time she took him to her apartment, a dirty East Village one-room decorated with batik shawls and teddy bears. And she kept hamsters, ratlike creatures whose bony feet scurried tirelessly on metal wheels: they must have been crazed with boredom, to go on like that, their minute eyes gleaming. After another session of frantic fucking (he couldn't possibly call it love-making), he and the girl had fallen into a clammy sleep. Suddenly, in the middle of the night, his eyes opened: the strange room; the window a rectangle of grey light; her body beside him warm, breathing; black hair flowing over small breasts. It must have been about four in the morning, nearly light enough for him to read the titles of the paperbacks on the table beside her pillow. He lay staring at the ceiling, wondering what had startled him out of sleep. Then he heard it, a steady 'squeak squeak squeak,' a dwarf's treadmill. With a tremor of revulsion he remembered her little rodents, and, hoisting himself up on an elbow, he saw, on the floor, one of the hamsters working its wheel with what seemed to him a terrible urgency: grim, inexhaustible, and as purposeless as undirected lust.

Now he said to Gwendolyn, 'Yes, I remember you.' He sighed. 'And what do you want of me now?'

She gave him a sidelong look. 'How's the painting going? Not too well, huh? I mean, I don't hear about you that much anymore. I guess you must have sort of dried up, right? Is it because you sold out? People are saying you sort of sold out. But I guess almost everyone sells out these days, right?'

He realised that she was trying to do what had worked before, provoke him with insults so that he might fuck her in anger. He wondered what kind of life she was leading these days. He vaguely remembered her telling him how bored she was at Pratt, and that she wanted to design jewellery (or was it textiles?) after she graduated. But he doubted if she was working at all now, and he suspected, with a chill, that she might simply have become an artist's groupie, content to move blithely from Ted Rubenstein's bed to his own, or anyone else's, as long as the guy was famous and trendy enough.

She suddenly mumbled in a surly voice, 'That redhead you were talking to last night, I guess she's your girlfriend.'

Ah, yes, Gwendolyn had seen him talking intently to Claire Browne. He was going to rebuke her, to tell her to mind her own business, but looking at her truculent face he realised that her particular kind of sharp sexiness might after all be a defence, maybe even a plea; underneath it she was probably just a hurt kid. 'No,' he answered gently, 'She's a friend of mine. Listen, Gwendolyn, you are a pretty young woman, but my life has changed...' He felt so pompous.

'Okay, okay,' she said brusquely, throwing her burnt-out cigarette on the floor, 'I get the fucking message.' She paused at the door. 'Hey, could I have some money? Just twenty bucks or something?'

Sighing, he went into the studio where he kept his wallet and came out with three ten-dollar bills, which he thrust into her hand. After she'd nestled them securely in the back pocket of her jeans, she measured him airily. 'By the way, Ted thinks you're a has-been,' she said, and closed the door behind her before he could answer.

# Chapter Eight

As a child Claire had listened, rapt, to her Jewish mother's stories about the Bronx, a different New York, how the rag man had trundled his barrow through the streets, and parents had called to their children from tenement windows. Her maternal grandparents had died before she was born, but she did remember her great-uncle Isaac, erect and thin with a blanched, sad face above impeccable suits, and his roly-poly wife, Tante Rachel, whose plump fingers had wrung her childish cheeks with merciless affection. She could still clearly recall Isaac and Rachel's Bronx apartment: the long corridors; the enormous kitchen; the dining table heaped with plates of boiled chicken, potato pancakes, noodle pudding, torn loaves of golden bread, tiny crystal glasses full of sweet, inky wine.

She often wondered what her father's Irish Protestant

family would have made of that table, of that overabundance of anaemic chicken and those minute glasses of Manishewitz and all that shouting and interrupting, Tante Rachel fastening her predatory fingers on your cheek or buttock and squeezing it to death. Conversely, she wondered how austere Isaac and frumpy Rachel would have felt at one of her paternal grandmother's decorous dinner parties. How would they have dealt with all those sedate guests drinking gin, nibbling canapés ('canopace?' she could hear Rachel ask), talking golf and stocks and bonds – Isaac and Rachel, for whom a dinner party had meant Trotskyists bellowing at Leninists over a rubble of *challah* and schnapps?

Actually they had never been asked to her other grandmother's East Seventy-fourth Street apartment, but she could picture them there, huddled in their dark clothes like the refugees they were, trying to swallow gin-and-tonics, smiling anxiously at haughty, bitchy Grandmother Fabienne. Claire had always loved Isaac with his sad dignity, his accent, his foolish loud wife. He and Rachel had come to New York straight from the *shtetl* with nothing but their poverty and Commie principles; they would have been gassed, most likely, had they remained in Russia. Yes, she had loved them both, and had always felt that her own father belonged by temperament more to them than to his own family...

\* \* \*

It had been raining, and now a muffled grey light shone through Simon's windows, reminding Claire of her old New York City public school on a wet day. Dripping raincoats; a smell of wool and chalk; and precisely this kind of milky light clouding in through the windows of that Victorian building, with its red stone and scrolled silver door handles. How memory threw things into relief!

She was on the floor near the bed, removing papers and books from a cardboard carton. Simon had said, 'Some of these boxes have been here for decades, and I'm embarrassed to admit that I have no idea what's in them, probably a jumble of letters and bills, I literally don't know, but I'm sure they're in no order at all. If you could arrange everything chronologically, and by category – just invent categories – then we'd at least be on our way out of chaos and into some kind of system. If it can be done, of course. Sometimes darkness and disorder seem the only visible light.' And he had grimaced.

She chose, at random, a sheet of typing paper on which was scrawled in blue ink:

*4 April '78. Girl at window. 1/2 face behind curtain. Light: deep gold (England, Olivia light) and green (green is expectant). She wants to begin to work again.*

She felt a quiver of excitement at this glimpse of Simon's process and intention. Next, she took up a blank envelope and removed a letter from it. The handwriting was different here, narrow and spidery:

*14 July 1979*

*Dear Simon,*

*I write this at two in the afternoon. It has been raining all day and the sky is full of pewter light.* [Claire glanced out again at the dull silver sky.] *Dr Curry keeps telling me I ought to paint and I say, yes perhaps, just to be agreeable, but really it makes me angry. All these dough-faced, sedated people finger-painting for therapy! But then again why should I be angry? I am also sedated, and when I looked in the mirror this morning I saw that my face has grown just as puffy as theirs, and my hair – Oh, Simon, my one vanity! – is now quite dull. So I mustn't insist that I am different from the others. But if I were to paint as they do, all of them frowning earnestly at the easel, silent and polite as though painting were a joyless duty, oh, if I were to do that, would I ever again be able to paint as my real self?*

*Anyway, don't worry about me, this place isn't too bad except for the food. As for old Curry, he has a face like an anvil but he is nice and eager to please. I suppose the hardest thing is loving you so much. Sometimes this blundering force of love in me cries, Why can't I just lose myself in him and he in me? Why must we live in separate skins? I should like to eat you up, do a great violence to you. (Of course, despite this nonsense, what I truly want is independence, which we have agreed is the source of love.)*

*So. I am determined to be less sad. Why have I always been so sad, Simon? Old Curry doesn't seem to know either. I do realise that I have disappointed you. When you first met me you probably thought that my glooms were some kind of romantic melancholy. You did, didn't you? Whereas they were only a kind of marsh-light.*

*There are some interesting characters here, as you can imagine. We actually have two Marilyn Monroes! Each thinks the other is an impostor, of course. The lady next door will only eat her meals in the bathroom.*

*I must go now because it is time to have another scintillating*

*session with Dr Curry. You are an excellent painter and a
prince amongst men.*

*Happy Bastille day, Olivia*

Claire took a deep breath. Then she straightened her shoulders
and read the next letter, which was typewritten on a piece of
yellow foolscap:

*22 Feb. 1982*

*Dear Olivia,*

*I am sorry but there are things you don't understand. It's
strange, as a serious young man I used to wonder about the
mystery of other people, about what it would really mean to
know someone else. Finally I decided that it would mean
knowing myself, it would mean terror and shame, throwing
off old protective skins, it would mean the electric shock of
another person's flesh and blood and bone. And it would
mean love, our only chance. You used to talk about drowning
in me, wanting to and yet resenting it. But you never understood. Our closeness relies on our separateness, the spaces
between us are what connect us. But you are not connected,
you in your corridor of mirrors. I have often wanted to paint
those silver webs that one sees at twilight in country places,
each filament discrete but bound up in the entire structure, a
silver floss draped across black trees. But I digress, and
besides, nobody in New York wants such delicacies as spider
webs at dusk...*

The letter stopped there. At the bottom of the page there was a jagged design in black ink, drawn deep and hard as though an angry hand had trawled the pen across the paper; the foolscap was punctured in two places. Claire inserted this and the previous letter into a folder, then took out her pencil, but stopped: how should she label this file? Olivia? That seemed presumptuous. Marriage? Domestic Issues? She finally settled for the whimsical and vague: Personal: Closeness/Separateness.

Simon had been right about the haphazard order of these materials; the next letter, while also from Olivia, was considerably older:

*12 April 1974*

*Dear Simon,*

*Terry loves my pictures, but there's no exhibition space at present. What an unpleasant business it all is, I don't know how you stand it. To be successful must be nearly as nasty as being at the bottom of the heap. Nicko and Jenny say hello.*

*Love, Livvy*

This was followed by a photocopy of a letter from Simon beginning *Dear O*, but Claire soon realised that the 'O' referred not to Olivia, but to Owen Kettlethorpe:

*3 Feb.*

*Dear O,*

*Just got your letter of 30 Jan. Very interesting. I am lucky to have you for a friend, since as you know I am really stupid about art history, the Baroque especially. Those paintings*

82

*had always struck me as murky compared to, say, Botticelli, whose pigments are so clear. But now thanks to you I see the period differently, Rembrandt, for instance, that quick gold light against the deep, deep shadow. I understand now that his light and darkness are not murky at all, but mysterious, even mystical. I'll have to learn more about it all, for my own sake. My God, Rembrandt! I think of him working in poverty, no glory, his face in those late self-portraits exhausted, impatient, nearly defeated, but still full of that extraordinary light. When I compare him to my esteemed colleagues, all the self-important charlatans who would do anything for a buck and a moment of attention, it sickens me. Well, I've done it too, I tried out that life of gimmickry and hijinks, and now – Jesus, I won't go into all that business again. What you say encourages me. I'll think hard about it. Happy New Year.*

*All the best, SB*

Underneath this were five old telephone bills, a few ancient party invitations and letters from galleries, then another Olivia letter, from 1983:

*Dear Simon,*

*You believe you are the king and we are all your subjects. You think everyone exists for your pleasure and that you can choose amongst people like objects, whichever one suits you. It is terrible to me how you gobble up the homage all those models and other girls give you, how you confuse your own self-regard with love for them, how it doesn't matter to you that you might be violating something precious. Speaking of your women, Bronwen told me everything...*

Claire stared out the window. The sun had emerged and now the rinsed sky glowed. It occurred to her that the work she was doing was like *pentimenti* on a canvas, layer after layer yielding up different truths and different fictions. Sighing, she was about to resume reading this last letter when suddenly, her fingers trembling, she re-folded it and thrust it into her handbag which was beside her on the floor.

For a moment she stared stupidly at her hands, as if they had filched the letter of their own volition. Then she said to herself, I'll just read it at home and return it tomorrow. No harm done.

Quickly, before she could allow herself to think about what she had done, she drew another letter from a blank envelope. A new handwriting:

*17 May 1977*

*My dear Simon,*

*It was wonderful to hear from you, my boy, especially as I know how busy you are these days, and how hard it is to phone. You did your old dad's heart much good.*

*I have read Tully's piece as you asked me to, and really, Simon, I don't think you should sweat about it. Tully is the sort who confuses his own personal grievances with matters of principle. If he himself had attained any success as an artist he would be seeing things differently now, but since he is a failure he has decided that all the current painters are corrupt, particularly those who have achieved precisely the things he wanted for himself. Let his disaffection be a lesson to you, my son, to prevent you from ever succumbing to that kind of spiteful nonsense. It seems to me that too many old men finish up in that state, full of bile and envy. You were always sensitive, Simon, which I believe gives you great power as an artist, but I guess it also means you remain vulnerable to vipers like Tully.*

*I try always to respect your sense of delicacy, which is why I didn't pursue the issue of your domestic problems on the phone last Saturday. However let me say now that I am sure things will work out. I have great confidence in both you and Livvy. You know, Simon, I never had a flair for psychiatry – when I had to do it in medical school I was a fish out of water, but it seems clear to me that Olivia is suffering from a clinical depression, and that what she needs is good professional help and a course of medication, and then you and she would be able to take it from there.*

*Anyway, that's enough for now from this old windbag, and forgive your father if he has been intruding. I enjoyed that wonderful review of your current show in the* Globe. *Hear from you soon.*

*Love, Dad*

There was a postscript:

*The heart is still stout, don't worry. Michaelson tells me to walk a lot and work in the garden and to give up sex and butter. I've agreed to everything but the last. What is life without butter?*

Beneath this there was a photograph, a close-up of a woman with long fair hair and a strong, handsome, slightly sad face. Olivia, surely?

Suddenly, behind her, Simon called, 'Claire, would you like some lunch?' She scrambled to her feet, feeling somehow guilty, as if she had been caught reading a stranger's correspondence, which of course she was doing, indeed was being paid to do.

\* \* \*

He had covered the dining table with a crimson cloth, and on it had arranged a plate of cheeses – a semicircle of ripe brie, a chunk of snowy goat's cheese, some crumbling Stilton, pieces of cheddar and gruyère – along with a basket of French bread, a bowl of salad gleaming with oil, and another bowl of grapes and the first peaches of the season. He had also opened a bottle of Côtes-du-Rhône.

Claire, faintly alarmed, said, 'How lovely. But I don't know if I should have wine. It might make me too bleary to work.'

He laughed. 'There's coffee afterwards.'

She accepted a glass. 'You are an epicure, Simon.'

He settled down next to her and broke a piece of bread from the basket. 'I like good food and drink, don't you?'

'Yes. And I love restaurants.'

'Why do you love restaurants?' She was again struck, as on their first meeting, by his forthright curiosity. It seemed he was never content to talk lightly; always he focused on your words with a dry intensity, even when you had spoken thoughtlessly. It was as though he believed that nothing in this world should remain unexamined – or else he was just flattering her. But she answered seriously, 'I love them because they are full of living life.'

He smiled over his wineglass, 'Living life, indeed? What

would that be when it's at home?' Then, peering at her, he asked, 'What was your adolescence like, Miss Claire Browne?'

Again a blunt, personal question, at once flattering and alarming, as well as slightly mocking. This time she decided *not* to answer seriously. 'My adolescence was marvellous, just like everybody else's.'

He eased back in his wicker chair and gave her a wry smile. 'Truly.'

'I was very dreamy, and solitary. I lived more richly in books than I did in the world.'

'Well, that helps to explain your somewhat eccentric sensibility.' He dipped his knife into the brie. 'Tell me more about your family.'

Because she had become, this morning, the custodian of his difficult truths, she now felt a charge in the air between them, as of unspoken intimacies. She realised that a seduction was taking place, but she could not have said who was seducing whom. She knew only that this moment seemed to deepen so that the time preceding it and the time that would come after were in eclipse; there was only this room and this man whose eyes were warming her more than the wine. She wanted to believe in him. She thought it was good that he had confided in her through the letters, and so she felt compelled to offer a confidence in return. 'My father is ill,' she said, 'but usually I don't talk about that.'

'You're talking about it now. How is he ill?'

She hesitated, then told him most of it, how her father had always been absent-minded, like so many professors, muttering to himself and walking into water-coolers, but then his forgetfulness had begun to worsen into something much more serious than mere absentmindedness...

'Were you close to him?'

'Yes, when I was small. I was so proud of him, of all the secrets he knew, the mysteries of the body, how babies were born and so on. I adored him.'

'And after you were no longer small?'

'My mother was an alcoholic and when she was drunk she would rage at me, and he didn't protect me. He was – excessively humble. He didn't believe he could be strong. He was always placating my mother and telling me to placate her.'

'Oh dear. No wonder you lived more fully in books than in life.' He poured them more wine. 'But it creates problems, doesn't it, when the world of your imagination is so much richer than the world around you?'

She laughed. 'You are an artist. You must know.'

He seemed to hesitate. 'When I was a kid my mother was ill all the time. They never explained why, my father and my aunts; they just told me to be quiet, so as not to disturb her, or they bustled me out of the house. So I went to the beach with my charcoals, even in bitter weather, and just drew all day long.' He looked beyond her, smiling slightly. 'Like you I was pretty solitary.'

*You were always sensitive, Simon.* She pictured him, a sullen boy on an empty beach, his hands grimy with charcoal, his heart breaking. She glanced at his hands now, curved lightly over the red tablecloth. Suddenly he extended a finger and touched her face. Hurriedly she said, 'They – they shouldn't have banished you from the house like that.'

'No. They shouldn't have banished me from the house.' He was still smiling. She knew that everything between them had changed now, subtly, delicately, the way daylight deepens into evening, or ash crumbles in a fire: an alteration of the air. Her skin seemed to throb where his finger had touched it. She swallowed. 'What was your mother ill with?'

'Cancer,' he said, then, gently, 'Listen, you can talk to me about your father any time.'

All of a sudden tears scalded her eyes and she looked away. 'I'm sorry,' she mumbled, 'It's just hard to let down the defences. And my home was often a place of shame, for me.'

After a pause he murmured, 'You interest me, Claire Browne. Sometimes you remind me of a startled forest creature. Or a character from some nineteenth-century novel – maybe Jane Eyre. Anyway, completely out of our present context.'

She brushed the back of her hand across her wet lashes. 'When I was a child I wanted to be like Jane Eyre.'

'Were you a prudish little girl?'

Suddenly a wafer of sunlight fell across the table, glinting on their wine bottle, now two-thirds empty. She nibbled on a grape. 'In my house,' she answered finally, 'there was no ease, or grace. I felt I had to *work* for love. My mother's affection was arbitrary. She could be sweet one minute, then suddenly cruel.' She glanced shyly at him, but he said, 'So you always had to appease your mother, and try to be good? To bargain for love from the big people?'

Claire gazed down at the table, the bread, the brie with its clothlike rind; a crescent of peach shone on his white plate. I'm happy, she thought. She looked back up at him. 'There was always a lot of tension, when I was a child. My grand-mother was mortified because her son had married a Jewish girl, and she was also ashamed of her own family, because her grandfather had come from France, but via Ireland, and he was half-Catholic. Maybe that's why *I* have been haunted by a love for Ireland all my life! Maybe I was rebelling against my heartless granny. Oh, but I was lonely, very lonely, as a child. My dreams were of a place where I would be loved even if I were gauche and stumbling...'

'More than that,' he broke in, 'more than that. A place where each of your imperfections would increase the love.'

She dragged her eyes away from his and looked out the window. 'But I don't know you,' she exclaimed softly.

His voice said, 'I am beginning to feel I know *you*, Claire Browne.'

Images of libraries came suddenly into her mind, scholars reading at long brown tables, the air brownish with dust, a projector throwing Caravaggio's paintings (garnet-coloured wine, bruised fruit, black hair shining against hot white faces) onto a dark wall. Why was she thinking of these things now? Was she trying to move away a little, right the balance? Did she fear that this man might draw her into his orbit as into a vortex, compelling her to drown her own dreams in some dream of him, some dream of a redemptive love? Had he made love to all his models, to his admirers and apprentices? What had gone wrong in his marriage? Suddenly she got up and walked over to the window. He followed her, but did not try to talk or touch her. They stared down at the street for a while; then he asked conversationally, 'Why do you like the Baroque so much?'

'Mostly because of the light. You described it in one of the letters I read today; you said you loved that interior glow in the Rembrandt self-portraits.'

'Yes. An inner light. And I love the pathos in Rembrandt, also.'

Once, as a child, she had observed her great-uncle Isaac

remove grapefruit pulp, too tough for false teeth, from his mouth, and place it on his plate with careful gestures. And somehow those gestures had broken her heart, the painstaking movements of his palsied hand, the grapefruit fibres on the corner of his dish. His innocence, dignity, fastidiousness... Pathos. Why had she talked to this stranger about her private loneliness? She realised that he was looking intently at her. He said, 'You know, it's mad, but I think I am already half in love with you.'

'It isn't possible,' she answered, her voice trembling. But as though he hadn't heard he took her face in his hands and kissed her. She thought about the letters she had read that morning, about Olivia's unhappiness, all his complicated history. Oh, God, she thought, What am I doing? But he had hoisted her up onto a small table and she couldn't help it, she was wrapping her legs around his waist as he pressed her close and kissed her on the mouth. Then, tipping her so that her head dropped back, he kissed her exposed throat and the hollow between her collarbones. She straightened her head then and looked out the window, to where clouds were coursing slowly across the rain-washed sky. He unbuttoned her blouse and pushed it back over her shoulders. 'You are as white as church marble,' he said, touching the tops of her breasts above her bra. 'Simon,' she whispered, and he swung her up in his arms and carried her into the bedroom.

He was slow and deliberate, and he asked her not to move, which at first made her uneasy, but when he prevailed on her to allow him to remove her clothes piece by piece and with each removal to caress the place he had revealed – so that soon he was stroking her all over, every plane, curve, and inlet of her body – then it was joy, it was every sweetness. Finally

91

he lay down and she straddled him, and kissed the dark cup beneath his throat as he had kissed hers, while his hands wandered down her spine and buttocks and thighs. A dry heat had flared up under his skin, and over this dryness a fine sweat was blooming, tangy on her lips. After a few moments he swung himself over her and stared down into her face.

'Oh, don't leave,' she heard herself say, 'Don't leave me now.'

'I won't,' he said, 'I won't leave.' Down below in the streets a car screeched and a child cried 'Angelo'. She closed her eyes and a long low groan drew itself out of her and she was away. But to where?

\* \* \*

She must have slept although she didn't remember. Through half-closed eyes she saw the smoke of his cigarette eddying into the sunlight. Presently, without speaking, he moved down on the bed until his head was between her thighs. Her legs fell open. His fingers touched her rough curls; she could feel his breath. Then he brought his face even closer, and in a sudden rush of desire she covered her eyes with her hands, and cried out. When she was spent he laid his head on her wet thigh until she stopped trembling.

They slept again, but this time she had a dream, that her father had taken her to a chapel in Ireland where a plaster Virgin was smiling above terraced candles. She opened her eyes with a start, to see Simon gazing down at her. He drew her left hand up to his mouth and kissed its palm.

'Claire,' he said, 'Claire.' Like a statement. The sunlight burned through two red glass bowls on a table by the window. She remembered her dream, candles wavering beneath the

Virgin's outspread arms; the weight of her father's hand in hers. Simon touched her shoulder. 'Claire, that first day you came here in your lavender dress, I knew we would eventually make love.'

She averted her eyes; she didn't know what she was feeling. His hand caressed her hair, and he went on, 'I imagine you have a lot to untangle in your life, and I don't want to complicate it further. Let's just take it easy, okay?' When she still did not answer he murmured, 'You know, very seldom have I felt called to attention by someone; very seldom has my desire for love been able to focus on a face, a voice...' She looked at him then and gingerly touched his cheek. He continued slowly, 'And when that happens, when one face out of all the faces in the world comes suddenly into focus...' His hand glided down her arm and over her hip. 'That first minute your big eyes looked at me, I knew we'd eventually make love, but I didn't know then how tender my feelings for you would become.'

A voice in her head was telling her to be wary, but other, hungrier voices implored her to believe his every word. She knew that she was too incautious, too romantic, too eager to throw herself into love, but at this moment she was full of both post-coital tenderness and foreboding. She did not want to fall in love with him just because her life was full of dreary sad things from which she believed he might rescue her. 'We should be careful,' she ventured.

'We will be careful. But it was lovely – wasn't it lovely? – what we did just now?'

In answer she nestled closer to him and kissed his lips, his cheek, his throat. They slept again, in each other's arms.

\* \* \*

She was gazing out the window, feeling happy, when suddenly, his mouth against her hair, he mumbled, 'Tell me about Caravaggio.'

She considered. 'Well, once he ordered a plate of artichokes at this restaurant in Rome.'

He laughed drowsily. 'They actually know what he ordered?'

'Hush. Listen. Caravaggio went swaggering into this restaurant, the Osteria del Moro, with his sword. It was bad manners to take your sword into a restaurant but Caravaggio was always spoiling for a fight. And he ordered eight artichokes, four cooked in butter and four in olive oil.'

'*Eight? One* artichoke takes about an hour to eat.!'

'They were the small delicious Italian artichokes that are fried in a pan and eaten whole. When the waiter brought him the plate, Caravaggio wanted to know which of the eight artichokes had been cooked in the butter and which in the oil. And the waiter cried, 'How the hell should I know? Smell them and you'll see.' So Caravaggio threw the plate of hot artichokes at him, and the poor waiter's cheek was scalded.'

Simon laughed again. 'So that's why you like me. I remind you of Caravaggio.'

'No. You remind me of artichokes.'

'Do you like artichokes?'

'Yes. Although you have to make your way through all those barbs before you reach the heart.'

'I have no barbs left,' he said quietly.

She touched him lightly all down his chest and stomach and then between his legs, and they made love again. Presently he went to the kitchen and came back with two glasses of brandy. 'That painting,' he said suddenly, 'that painting by Carlos Moreno – Owen has brought it to New York.'

Her heart gave a thump but she remained very still, balancing her brandy glass in both hands, while he told her that Owen Kettlethorpe had travelled from Paris to New York with this possible Moreno, which he had placed in the suite of rooms that he kept in some posh Madison Avenue hotel.

'*Why* has he brought the painting to New York?' she asked.

'Owen told me that if it is indeed authentic he would like to sell it to a particular man here. I don't know who this man is, a museum curator, probably, or maybe a private collector. Owen said he's still unsure if the picture is a fake or not. I don't think he wants to subject it to radiation, or to any of those other high-tech methods they use now.' He paused. 'I was thinking you should go with me, to Owen's hotel, to help him authenticate it.'

She stared at him, too astonished even to protest. He went on easily, 'It's still a secret from most of the art world, but I asked Owen about you, and he agreed that you should be brought in. He knows your work, of course, and he thinks you are a fine writer and that you have a real scholarly mind – those were his exact words.'

She took a gulp of brandy, which scorched her throat so that she fell into a paroxysm of coughing. Ignoring this, Simon went on, 'I kept thinking about it, how wonderful it would be for your career if a great art expert were so impressed with your talent and intelligence that he asked you to help him authenticate a Baroque painting, and then you wrote about it for *ArtDimension* as an exclusive story, a scoop.' He sipped from his glass. 'So, he said that we should meet for a meal some night soon, and then go to his hotel and have a look at this Moreno – or fake Moreno, as the case may be.' He placed his glass on the bed table and laced his fingers behind his head.

'It would be fascinating,' she said wonderingly, 'a marvellous kind of sleuthing.' She paused, realising she was blushing with confusion and happiness. 'Simon! I– really, this is extraordinary. Owen Kettlethorpe, Jesus! And the painting. How much do you know about it?'

'Not a thing. I don't know its name or subject. Owen promised he'd explain everything when we met. I thought we might have dinner with him next week.'

'I don't know how to thank you,' she said in a low voice. 'I feel a bit scared, the way one does when things are too lovely, as though to be so happy is a kind of *hubris*.'

He laughed. 'But the gods are delighted by love. Don't worry about appeasing them; we have already made them an offering, through what we are feeling, and what we have expressed: pleasure, gratitude, love.'

Love! How her foolish, virgin-in-a-bower heart jumped at that old word, uttered so blithely by that rueful, talented, alien mouth. She was still optimistic enough to think that love was the thing, love the skein we could spin from ourselves into the rich strange heart of some other. But what was in store for her now? Those old clichés: the vigils by the phone, the fear and doubt and hunger? Ah, but he had ignited her, she was already burning, it was too late. Looking at his tousled hair, his face, she could not deny it, I love you, she thought. Then, Oh, what an idiot you are, Claire Browne.

# Chapter Nine

Walking home from Simon's loft, she remembered a morning at Atocha Station in Madrid, when she was on her holiday in Spain with Jeremy.

Arriving early for the eleven o'clock AVE to Seville, they had decided to stop for a croissant and a *café con leche*. But Jeremy had gone off to collect their tickets, leaving her alone at a small table, where she was content to look at her neighbours: a weary mother with three small children; a young man clutching his ticket and talking intently to a beautiful girl in a black coat; an elegant woman eating a *bocadillo*. And an old man, fumbling over his cup, large with thin grey hair and a pallid complexion. It was his eyes that arrested her, dark, startled, cowled with old flesh: they were her father's eyes.

It was the same as when one sees a child all by himself in

some quiet park at twilight, crying and afraid; now this large old man alone in an indifferent café, with his clean raincoat, scant grey hair, fumbling hands – and those eyes, terrified as though before an abyss.

She looked away from him, up at the station's great glass ceiling. Filmed in sunlight, it seemed nearly to be floating, an airy carapace, but she imagined that on a rainy day it would appear ominous, throwing a bruised-looking darkness into these vast spaces, and compelling people to hurry along like passengers on a stormy sea. Then she glanced again at the old man.

A young waitress was being kind to him, bending down to examine the coins he was proffering in his trembling hand. So he was not too far gone, not yet. He could still travel, venturing alone into this immense station, buying a coffee at the café (even if he did have to ask for help with the coins), buying his ticket. Now he had produced the ticket from his mackintosh pocket. The waitress looked at it and smiled. No, he was not yet too far gone. Ah, but those perplexed eyes in a face slack with worry, like a face which has just been struck. She knew what it meant, she knew what it meant.

The man was laughing up at the waitress, and touching her hand on the table; it was clear that he did not want her to go, even though the café was nearly full. He was making a clumsy attempt at gallantry, at the kind of jaunty flirtatiousness elderly men sometimes affect with young women, chuckling, touching her hand, but the smile wavered, the old fingers shook...

Again she looked at the high ceiling, vaults groined as a cathedral. As an American, and a half-Jew, European stations had always seemed to her at once romantic and menacing, full of soldiers, refugees, and anxious couples rushing along platforms in an ultramarine darkness while steam hissed from black engines. But today Atocha Station was clean and modern as an American shopping centre, and as ghostless.

What are you doing, staring up at the sky?' asked Jeremy irritably. He had come back with the tickets, and was frowning down at her. 'You haven't even asked for the bill yet, have you? It would be great, wouldn't it, to miss the AVE because as usual you were daydreaming?'

'I'm sorry.' Should she tell him about the old man, about her ancestral memory of European stations, about the kind of pity which, like love, can buckle the knees, weaken the stomach, scald the eyes? No, for he would only say – and rightly – that they should consider the practical things first... His impatience with her was nearly as great as her own.

\* \* \*

Simon had asked her not to leave, had suggested that they dine at the SoHo Charcuterie, and that she sleep over. She had listened to these proposals with some longing, but she had also felt, as on the night of Ted Rubenstein's party when she had declined his invitation to go out walking, that she must not hurtle into his life, or forsake her own, like Persephone taking the magic kernel which would keep her in thrall to Hades. It was not that she didn't want to, because she did, she did. Her whole imagination swayed towards it, towards this loft full of his things, towards his voice with its faint New England accent and ironical inflexions, towards his forearms, the round bone of his wrist, his square palms, the slightly peppery smell of his skin, towards the things they would do if she did remain here, how they would talk and drink and make love again, all within the strangeness of this new place. And her separate self was eager but afraid, happy but mournful, rejoicing but grieving, also, for the loss of its repose, for she would not be still, now, not for a while. So she had said no, no, she would go home, and do a bit of her own work. Besides, she hadn't a change of clothes, and she would be seeing him tomorrow, anyway.

Down in the street she was surprised by the brightness, the bustle of cars; she had expected darkness, somehow, a mutter of traffic, but it was spring and not yet dusk. In Washington Square the fountain threw streamers of spume that flashed in the sunlight, and boys slouched up beside her as she walked, offering to sell her drugs in crooning, seductive voices. A breeze blew her hair into her face and she smelled Simon on it; her hair, her skin, had absorbed him – the odour of his sperm, like straw or wet earth.

On Second Avenue she stopped at a deli to buy milk; then walked south, past the bazaar of Saint Mark's Place with its hawkers of ancient porn magazines, plundered shoes, and broken radios. On Sixth Street a tall woman wearing a scarlet dress glided by with a recumbent ostrich in her arms. It's good to be back in the East Village, Claire said to herself. She often felt the downtowner's disdain for that more genteel world north of Fourteenth Street, with its geometric avenues, boring shops, and office towers full of boring people wearing boring suits, as though it were another country. She also had the East Villager's wariness of the West Village and SoHo, since their gentrification was bound to engulf even Alphabet City, indeed had already begun to do so.

At home she moved restlessly, straightening cushions,

opening windows. She paused at her desk to study a photo of Moreno's 'Saint Catherine'. Again she was struck by Catherine's passionate expression, how some erotic force seemed to surge in her wild hair and to flare from her dark eyes. She was flinging her right arm forward, in invitation or entreaty, while her left hand clutched a brown robe to her thick white bosom. The slightly awkward fingers of that hand had given the experts some trouble, as had the painting's brushwork, which was at some variance with Moreno's usual paint-laden brush, his opulent thickness. 'Thin,' one French curator had pronounced, 'thin and wan. *Not* Moreno's style at all. Furthermore,' he had continued impatiently, 'the girl is simply too sexy, with that robe falling off her shoulders!'

This curator had wanted to subject the picture to radiography. But Owen Kettlethorpe and Claire, writing independently of each other, had come to the same conclusion: according to legend Saint Catherine had undergone a mystical marriage to Christ, and Moreno, a humanist, must have wanted to express this mystical union in human terms, to convey that Catherine's love for God had fired the whole web of her humanity, every strand, even the sexual. And in a direct salvo to the French curator Kettlethorpe had insisted that the painting's brushwork was indeed thick enough to be Moreno's, and that the crackle pattern looked authentically haphazard; surely the 'Saint Catherine' must be genuine?

Catherine had been the patron saint of Zoë's Louisiana high school, so Zoë knew all about her. She had told Claire, 'That girl said she would not sleep with the king because she was the bride of Jesus. Honey, can you believe how those fourth-century virgins talked? Imagine being fool enough to die for your hymen. It is much harder to live, and love, like a human.'

Now Claire smiled, and called Zoë, who said groggily, 'Hi, baby. I am just back from entertaining a vitamin company president called Chester at his suite in the Sherry Netherland. Those vitamins give that man a lot of energy. How are you?'

Claire told her about her afternoon, remembering to leave out any mention of Owen Kettlethorpe and the painting, since Simon had asked her not to talk about it. She spoke instead about her feelings and about how Simon had made love to her. 'I am trying to be slow and careful, Zoë,' she sighed, 'but it's hard.' Then, knowing she would seem *jejune* and coy, but unable to help herself, she exclaimed, 'Oh, I suppose I am half in love with him – is it wise, Zoë?'

There was a brief silence. Then Zoë gave her deep laugh. 'I don't know, baby. What *I* have with men is always a fantasy. Almost every night I meet some businessman in his fancy hotel room. He gives me champagne and I fire him up and then he makes me into his own particular private dream. Why, honey, just last week I diapered a senior senator, and this priest who is my regular client always asks me to beat him with his breviary beads. I am drawn into every possible dream that there is, I sometimes think. Did you know that because of my *café au lait* complexion and being from Louisiana, a lot of men ask me to pretend that I am some sweet Creole girl in a New Orleans whorehouse? When I first came to New York and was working at the escort service my boss's name for me was "Miss Zoë Martin, Octaroon Beauty from New Orleans." Well, there is a long tradition of that kind of thing in New Orleans, so I didn't mind. I can get into almost anything. But I don't pretend it's real.'

'Your boyfriend, Beauregard, that was real?'

Another pause. 'It became real, but, you know, at first it

was just so romantic, because he was a musician and every-thing. The *really* real thing does not come along too often, honey. That's why it is so precious.'

* * *

That night she couldn't sleep. For some reason she was thinking of Spain again, how she had gazed out the window on that journey on the AVE from Madrid to Seville, at goats clambering down a rocky slope, fallow fields under a sun-bleached sky, dusty acres covered with some sere plant she couldn't name; then, further south, glimpses here and there of vineyards and gardens, their greenness as soothing to the eye as water to a parched throat.

Jeremy seldom looked out the window, but immersed him-self in *The International Herald Tribune,* muttering about Reagan and his cronies. The AVE throbbed like a plane and on the television monitor John Wayne, as Townsend Harris in *The Barbarian and the Geisha*, was talking in Spanish to a Japanese woman, who answered him in Spanish. As they slowed to enter Cordoba she saw more particulars of the landscape: an orange tree with glossy leaves, a distant church tower, two boys walking through a dry field. 'Hollywood movies in Spanish,' she said to Jeremy, 'And just out there, goats and old churches and orange trees, if anyone bothered to look.'

'Postmodernism,' Jeremy mumbled, scowling at a photo of Margaret Thatcher, 'Layer upon layer of images, made shallow by their sudden juxtaposition, until they are drained of meaning, and you of feeling.'

She squeezed past him to go to the toilet, where she glanced at herself in the mirror, at her eyes which were usually auburn, but sometimes amber or chestnut, depending on the light. Those who preferred strength and elegance in women's faces were unmoved by hers, but it had pleased her father, who used to call her an overgrown imp, before he got sick. Suddenly and for no apparent reason she realised that all through her early life she had thought she had feared outward perils, snipers in university towers, men offering sweets in the park, dogs who might be rabid, when all along the things that had really scared her were in the house with her, they always had been there, breathing beside her, the rancorous voice of her mother, a dish shattering against a wall, the air darkening, her father never any help, and now... She pressed her forehead against the mirror.

Now she couldn't sleep at all. She got out of bed and walked around her tiny apartment. Already there was a glint of dawn in the air. She went into the kitchenette and made herself a cup of tea, in the half darkness.

Being *in love*, she knew, was different from love. Being in love was like having a fever. It heightened and distilled things, it made life *thrum*, but it could guarantee neither grace, nor sweetness, nor joy. Real love, if it was, as she believed, life's only true redemptive force, could provide all those things. She also knew that essentially she was strong, and would come through, somehow, no matter what. But something in her did not seem to want her to come through, compelled her, even, like the low seductive voices she had heard today in Washington Square crooning, 'Coke crack grass smack,' to lose herself.

While she drank her tea her eyes moved over the walls, the counter, her handbag on the other chair, transformed by shadow into a sleeping beast...

Slowly she took the bag onto her lap and rummaged in it

for the letter she had placed there.

After putting on the light, she smoothed the pale blue sheet out on the table, and Olivia's jagged writing jumped up at her:

*20 April 1983*

*Dear Simon,*

*You believe you are the king and we are all your subjects. You think everyone exists for your pleasure and that you can choose amongst people like objects, whichever one suits you. It is terrible to me how you gobble up the homage all those models and other girls give you, how you mistake your own self-regard for love of them, how it doesn't matter to you that you might be violating something precious. And speaking of your women, Bronwen told me everything about your sordid affair with her last year in California. (She assured me that her confidences were for my own good, of course.) She told me that you talked to her a great deal about your troubled marriage, about my depressions, about the death of our sex life. So you have betrayed me not only with your body but by telling our intimate story to these women.*

*Once when you were shouting at me you said that I did not know how to love, that the only things I could attach to were my own woes, that for me other people were just projections from my own psyche, that I never really understood you. Perhaps you are right, I do not know, but I did try to love you, Simon, and it seems to me that you never knew or understood me, either. I suppose we both made a sorry muddle of things, but all I can say now is that you have disappointed me deeply, and at this point I simply do not want to be wrecked by you, I do not want to go back to*

105

*hospital again, I do not want to give up. So I have to re-
nounce you. Please don't ring me, I need to keep my strength.
I will not talk to you.*

There was no signature. Claire returned the letter to her bag
and went back to bed. This time, for some reason, she fell
instantly asleep.

# Chapter Ten

A fter Claire left, Simon stood at the window. The loft felt very still; out in the street a woman in a yellow dress was walking a poodle. A man sauntered past, carrying a baguette, and the woman extended her hand to him; he stopped to talk with her, laughing, while the dog tried to scramble up his leg for the bread.

Suddenly Simon wanted to paint, wanted it so badly that his arms trembled. He went into the studio and began to lay out colours: that jonquil-coloured dress, the man's russet trousers, the white dog, the baton of bread, the gesture she had made, extending her arm to him. He painted, dry-mouthed, for a while, he did not know how long. Then he stopped, swallowing, and left the room without looking at what he had done.

He stared at the tousled bed. He missed her. Should he call

her now, just to see how she was? He laughed at himself; he was behaving like an adolescent. She would be coming back tomorrow morning.

Still afraid to look at the new canvas, he walked slowly into the kitchen and poured himself a glass of white wine. He did not know what was happening. He went to the red sofa and placed his glass on the coffee table. Then he just sat for a while, staring down at his hands, which, yesterday, had seemed to him so useless.

He was thinking, among other thoughts, that of all the things Claire had told him today – all about her exotic French-Irish-Jewish family, about her early loneliness so curiously like his own, about her father – out of all those confidences the one that clung most vividly in his memory was a comment she had made about being 'a child of the seventies'.

They were discussing the harsh conservatism which had engulfed America and England in the eighties, under Reagan and Thatcher respectively – that terrible twosome – when Claire suddenly said, 'I feel peculiar sometimes, being a member of my generation, after all the rebellions of the sixties. I was a child when the sixties were happening, the campuses erupting, the Beatles, all that, and it felt so exciting and lovely, but then it disappeared, all of a sudden, like snow off a rope, or so it seemed. And I felt *indignant*; why had they taken it all away, all the activism and music and poetry and wildness, just when I was coming of age? But I'm also old enough to have seen the dark face of the sixties, and to have lived through their aftermath – the dissipated, boring seventies– when I was in college, and the dream had gone wrong. I suppose that in the seventies I saw the sexual revolution collapse, I saw how the dream of free love can sour if it means that people stop caring about each other. Maybe that's one of the reasons I have lived too much in the past, in the world of old paintings. I was afraid, you see, of what was happening, the crazy parties where everyone just wanted to get plastered and stoned, the music no longer full of courage and intelligence, the *unconsciousness...* No-one was radical anymore, and it had become uncool to love too much. You were supposed to be casual about sex. Anything else was gauche and *wrong...*'

Now, again, Simon examined his hands, backs and palms. They never looked clean, even though he scrubbed them raw with carbolic soap. Paint had soaked into the skin, eaten into the furrows of the palms, darkened the seams across the knuckles. Once, at some sedate uptown dinner party, his hands had disconcerted a wealthy French lady, who had said dryly to him, 'Your face is fair and elegant, but you have the hands of a labourer.'

Twilight was approaching, a certain powdery blue, as though by some alchemy the light were becoming smoke. He felt three simultaneous impulses, to look at the new painting, to get drunk, and, once again, to call up Claire.

* * *

Instead, he went out for a walk, and saw Patrick O'Dwyer on Greene Street, staggering along with an enormous painting balanced on his shoulder. He had met Patrick at the Ear Inn last February, and had immediately liked him, this dark-eyed forthright Irishman, with his rasping smoker's laugh, wry manner, and sculptor's way of moulding the air with his hands while he talked. He was a struggling sculptor who had come to New York from Ireland two years before. Unable to break through in this hype-mad age, despite his obvious talent, he had taken a job with an art moving company, and Simon had grown used to seeing him all over SoHo, ferrying canvases in and out of galleries.

That first meeting at the Ear Inn, Simon had told Pat how much he loved Ireland. He had gone there first on a holiday, with Olivia, and when the plane approached Shannon he had looked out at the dawn sky and marvelled: The light is different. He had never really liked the light in America, bright as metal, whitening the skies. But this Irish sky was a luminous bowl with washes of gold, pewter, blue, an inward radiance as though the plane had turned upside-down and he were looking not at the sky at all but into sun-struck water.

Patrick O'Dwyer, drinking Guinness and smoking Players, had listened with a rueful smile to Simon's rhapsodic account, before declaring that it was fine and dandy for the famous Simon Brady to adore foreign lands, but as for himself, New York was *it*, the place to be. He was exhausted, working for the art movers and trying to get his own sculptures exhibited somewhere, anywhere in Manhattan. 'Only I'm not giving up,' he'd assured Simon, 'because the centre of the world is *here*. And I can't believe that the pig swill passing itself off as art these days will take over forever.' But he'd looked doubtful.

Now, noticing Simon, Pat hoisted the huge canvas off his shoulder and put it up against a car. 'Hello, Brady,' he said, breathing heavily. 'Jesus, isn't it a fucking pity that just as I accept a job moving art, paintings are getting bigger and bigger? It'd be grand if they would only give me some *normal*-sized pictures to carry, but these fucking things are all meant for *board rooms* and fucking *banks*. I was hauling a Schnabel across Eleventh Street yesterday and I nearly got knocked down by a van, which I couldn't see because the bloody canvas was so fucking *gigantic*. And then the van driver called me a goddamn sonofabitch. What a city!'

Together they regarded this new painting, which was all lashings of colour, green and white, with orange dribbles, and the word PIG — MENT scrawled across it in black. 'Ugly,' volunteered Pat, 'but it does resemble the Irish Tricolour, which redeems it a bit, maybe. I'm bringing it over to that pretentious little snool at the Carlyle Gallery. We didn't bother to package it up – it seemed too much trouble for such a piece of shite. The artist's name is Black Widow. I'm serious, look at the signature. Perhaps you'd fancy a pint later, at Fanelli's or the Ear Inn?'

'I'd like that,' Simon answered, gratefully. Again he was missing Claire acutely, and would appreciate the distraction.

* * *

Next morning Simon welcomed Claire with breakfast – boiled eggs, brown Irish soda bread, butter and raspberry jam, and the good stout coffee. At first she was full of a faltering, adolescent shyness, but when he suddenly caressed her cheek across the table, she relaxed, and it occurred to her that he might also be shy.

She worked in the morning, reading a number of arid documents from lawyers and accountants and the IRS; she couldn't understand their jargon, but the figures they threw around astonished her. Then she read a moving, grief-stricken diatribe written by a professor friend of Simon in 1980, just after Reagan's election:

*Paint, Simon, paint your rage and pain, paint the enemy out of their complacency. They are convinced that their hardness is alertness, that their moral cowardice is good business sense, that their cynicism is sophistication. We have elected a government of psychopaths...*

And it amused her to read a more recent letter from a super-fashionable painter called Ian Collins, whom Claire had met once through Darby Holland. She had liked him, and was happy to learn that his epistolary style was as uproarious as his conversation:

*Dear Kiddo,*

*You are a jerk, a boob, a provincial dummy, what am I going to do with you? Ah, I have the answer, I'll throw you into the Modern or the Guggenheim during one of those pretentious parties where wheeler-dealers drink disgusting wine and talk about how wonderful they are all night, now isn't that just what you deserve for being a stupidhead and not listening to your sweet friend who loves you enough to drive – to drive! – over to your dreary loft at 2 in the fucking morning last month for the sole purpose of informing stubborn you that LO is the worst dealer in NY? Anyway, you learned your lesson, Smartypants. Want some real news? I've met a woman here called Tibet, I'm telling the truth. She has red hair down to her knees and she's forty years old, really. I'm sick of little girls, Simon, this Tibet is a genuine human being and she's encouraging me to develop my artistic skills. I'm trying to convince her to come back to New York with me.*

Lunch was vegetable soup, sourdough bread, a salad of Italian lettuces and avocado in a lemony sauce, and a bottle of Chianti. She had contributed dessert, plum cakes from a French bakery on Prince Street, after which Simon poured them a measure each of cognac.

When he kissed her his mouth was fragrant with plums, and his skin was hot and dry all over, as though the brandy had ignited him. She, on the other hand, was completely water; the moment he touched her, sweat prickled out all over her body, her eyes misted, moisture flowed onto her thighs.

Later, while they were drowsing, she heard him mumble, 'Oh, God.'

'Don't name-drop,' she murmured against his arm.

He laughed. 'I just remembered that I forgot to tell you something. Owen would like us to come for dinner tomorrow night. And to see the painting. Are you free?'

'I don't know; I'll have to consult my busy social calendar. There might be a lively soap opera on television I'd hate to miss. *Of course* I'm free!'

# Chapter Eleven

Claude Caron, a rotund, bullet-headed man who had a grumpy demeanour in photographs, was a prosperous member of the Parisian bourgeoisie. When he died in 1924, he bequeathed his rue de Saint-Pères apartment to Caroline Prudhomme, his mistress. According to Owen Kettlethorpe, who had seen some rare pictures of her, Mademoiselle Prudhomme was an eccentric-looking woman with a lot of wild grey hair, sharp eyes small as currants, and a penchant for dusty black clothes which, in combination with her glaring face, gave her the look of an angry and dishevelled nun. Always a bit of a crackpot, she became a sour hermit after Caron's death, barricading herself in his flat against the throngs of art experts and curators who had heard about Caron's collection of Baroque painting. Smelling plunder, they made daily pilgrimages to Mademoiselle Prudhomme's door, where they cajoled, implored, threatened, blustered, wept. But this small creature told them all that Caron had expressly instructed her not to let vultures such as themselves soil his collection with their venal paws (he'd had a flair for the mixed metaphor), and so she was refusing to allow anyone in to see his treasures, and that was that. She died just before the Second World War, and by that time the collection was forgotten.

Monsieur Caron and Mademoiselle Prudhomme had a daughter, Claudine. In contrast to her art-worshipping father and eccentric mother (and perhaps as a reaction to having been born outside society), Mademoiselle Claudine was a stolid, conservative lady. She had inherited Caron's flat from her mother, and lived there currently with her husband, who had always encouraged her robust distaste for her father's unsuitable pursuits such as his picture collecting. The paintings hadn't even quickened this couple's mercenary appetite; Claudine, who apparently had her own reasons for resenting her father, refused to believe that any personal project of his could be either lucrative or respectable. As far as she was concerned the paintings were a burden and obscurely shameful. So she and her husband had agreed long ago to keep the collection in a sealed-off room, where they wouldn't even have to look at it.

Monsieur Caron had been an energetic man. In addition to housing his mistress and art collection on the raffish Rive Gauche, he had maintained a wife and children in a more decorous arrondissement across the river. Emile was an issue of this marriage. An affluent businessman in his own right, he travelled a great deal to England, where Owen Kettlethorpe had met him, at some party in London, after which they had become remote friends.

Recently Emile had stumbled on references to an art collection in his grandfather's letters. He hadn't known anything previously about Caroline Prudhomme or the flat in the rue de Saint-Pères, but after reading of Monsieur Caron's concealed Left Bank life – and his paintings – he decided to call on Claudine and to try and persuade her to let him look around.

How he prevailed on her Kettlethorpe didn't know, but finally she escorted him into the room where her poor father's pictures had been housed in darkness for so long, like some prurient secret, and allowed him to examine the canvases. Emile was no art expert, but he was astute enough to recognise that while some of the pictures were dross (mawkish, clumsy), others were, perhaps, valuable. Still, a mediocre collection on balance, he decided ruefully, cleaning the dust from his hands.

One last look perhaps? And then, as if it had been evading him all this time, he unearthed a painting of – what was the myth? – which made him, literally, gasp. He stared at the picture for a long time; then announced to his half-sister Claudine that she very likely had a precious work of art on her hands. Then he called Owen Kettlethorpe.

'And so here we are,' said Kettlethorpe, spreading his hands. He was telling this story to Simon and Claire over dinner in a shockingly expensive restaurant just east of Madison Avenue. They had already eaten lobster pate and drunk a bottle of Meursault, and now they were eating veal with morels and drinking Corton Charlemagne, a white wine so delicious and strong that it made Claire's eyes close with pleasure.

She thought she liked Owen Kettlethorpe. He was tall and loose-limbed, with a practised smile. The dull patina of privilege glowed on his silver hair and fine English suit, and his gestures were unfailingly elegant. He had beautiful large pale hands with long fingers. She supposed he was about fifty.

Swirling the last of the wine in his glass he said, 'Emile and Claudine didn't want to alert the curators at the Louvre, or anything like that. For all we know the French museums might have declared that the picture was their national treasure, even though it was painted by a Spaniard who had lived in Italy! For that matter, the Italian and Spanish museums could have done the same; so of course the Carons decided that this matter should be handled discreetly, through private channels. That's where I came in. I was even thinking of buying it for my own collection, but if the painting is genuine I know a collector in New York who would offer a *staggering* sum for it. I don't want to say too much about it before you see it, but I will tell you the subject.' He paused while the waiter removed their plates. 'Greek. Its title is "Echo and Narcissus."'

Claire gave a little jump, and the two men smiled enquiringly at her. She said, 'It's just that I am particularly fond of that myth, I suppose because it's so psychologically rich, so full of voices and silences and reflections. The story is awfully moving, I think.'

Owen asked Simon, 'Do you know it?'

They were served small salads and a fluid camembert, along with a bottle of red wine called St Amour.

Simon answered, 'I know that Narcissus is the boy who looks at himself in a pool, but I can't recall much about Echo.'

'Hah!' said Owen gloatingly, 'You ignoramus.'

Simon gave Claire a grin. 'Owen likes to pretend that I'm a barbarian who knows nothing about culture.'

'It's true,' responded Owen blandly, 'You might as well

admit it, you're an idiot *savant*. You know how to slop paint onto canvas but in every other area of life you are beyond hope.' To Claire he said, 'Since he has exposed his ignorance, why don't you tell him the story?' She hesitated, but he smiled, 'Please, Claire. You say you love the myth; I'd like to hear your interpretation of it.'

She swallowed some wine, considering. 'Well, let's see. Artemis, the moon and hunter goddess, had an entourage of nymphs who accompanied her on the chase, and among them was Echo. Echo was very pretty and pleasant, but she did have one fault. She loved to talk, and so she was always driving everyone mad with her incessant gabbling. Anyway, one day the jealous goddess Hera was stalking her husband Zeus, who had gone off frolicking with some nymphs. Hera stumbled on Echo who waylaid her and began chattering, as was her custom, and in this way she distracted Hera until Zeus could make his escape. Hera realised soon enough what Echo had done, and so she confronted her and said, "Listen Echo, you might think you are clever, but you shouldn't play around with the gods. Since you love to talk so much, I'll give you the last word, but that is all you will ever have from now on. From this day forward you will be unable to speak first; you'll just helplessly repeat the last phrase spoken to you." And this is how Echo was punished.'

Claire ate a piece of the camembert, and drank more wine. 'Now Narcissus comes in. He was an extremely beautiful youth who liked to hunt, so the nymphs were used to glimpsing him in the forests.'

'He was beautiful?' asked Simon. 'What did he look like?'

'According to Bullfinch he had curly hair, round cheeks, and an ivory throat.'

Simon said to Owen, 'That's the kind of thing only Claire would know.'

Owen grunted, '*My* Narcissus doesn't look like that.' He touched his lean face. 'Bullfinch probably had curls and fat cheeks.'

'Anyway,' continued Claire, 'Echo saw him one day and became immediately infatuated with him because he was so lovely. But she was voiceless, so all she could do was hover around waiting for him to speak first so she could answer him. She was in thrall, you know, without her own voice to express her love with, which I suppose could serve as a metaphor for how people feel when they're infatuated, all helpless and dumbstruck. Presently Narcissus noticed her and called, "Who's there?" And Echo said, "There." And then he said, "Who are you?" And she said, "You." So he thought she was crazy, which I suppose is understandable considering her behaviour, but I still suspect that Narcissus suffered from a certain poverty of imagination. He said to her, "Go away. I'd rather die than you should have me." And poor Echo could only answer forlornly, "Have me." She knew such anguish after that, she sickened and wasted away until only her voice remained. You can hear it still, in forests and caves and places like that, repeating the last thing you've said.'

The waiter appeared with coffee and balloon glasses of armagnac. Claire went on, 'So stupid old Narcissus, not knowing what he'd done, came one day to a clear pool. He looked down into it and saw the face of a beautiful youth. "You are so lovely," he said to the face, "I love you; talk to me." But the face was as mute in its fashion as Echo had been. He extended his hands to touch it, but they met only water, and the face dissolved, only to appear again a second later, but still it wouldn't answer him. Narcissus went mad with grief because the sweet youth was so close but so cruelly unattainable. And so he died, and the gods transformed him into a purple flower as a tribute to his beauty. The nymphs were very sad, especially Echo of course, and they mourned him and keened for him.'

'So he could love only himself,' Owen reflected.

Claire stirred her coffee. 'I don't think he loved himself. How could he love himself? He didn't know himself. When he looked at himself he thought it was someone else. He was completely marooned from himself.'

'Interesting,' said Simon, narrowing his eyes, 'the modern idea of narcissism. People do confuse it with self-love, don't they?'

'But it's not, I think,' answered Claire. 'It seems to me that narcissism is the opposite of self-love, although I suppose you could call it self-regard. It means you go around seeing everyone as a reflection or an extension of you, or something, and so you can love neither others nor yourself. You can't connect because you have no distinct life in which someone else's life might resonate – you're just lost, gazing into the pool.'

Owen said, 'Some people believe narcissism is an epidemic these days. Curious, in Freud's day everyone was afflicted with hysteria, ladies swooning and believing that they were paralysed and so forth, and today all these people are walking about utterly self-absorbed.'

'The walking wounded,' said Simon, lashing back the last of his brandy, 'Drowning in the hype of their own image, unable to love...'

# Chapter Twelve

The background depicted that hour towards dusk when the sky is washed with a pale light but objects against it are beginning to darken. There were mother-of-pearl clouds, and, below them, a wood, burdened with shadow, the trees ink-black as though by exhaling all that shadow into the sky they would themselves create the night.

The foreground was taken up by a wide pool. Flowers clustered at its border; watercress spilled into the silver water. Claire could nearly smell it, the peat-smell of a cool lake at twilight. Narcissus, on his knees, was staring not at his reflection but out at us, as was his echo in the water. His hair tumbled over his white brow in opulent black curls. His large dark eyes burned like lamps; they were full of desolation, and his mouth was half-open in a kind of grimace, as though he were about to cry out. His hands were flush on the ground, his arms and legs bare, his torso loosely swathed in a short white toga. He was bathed in an iridescence so rich it looked nearly molten. It was most intense on his face; then softened and darkened as it moved down along his body, but enough glowed around his knees to burnish the flowers at the lip of the pool, to deepen the yellows to saffron, kindle the greens to emerald, and redden the reds so that they shone like blood. The light glowed most faintly on Narcissus' mute reflection in the water.

Echo reflected him almost as closely as his own image. She was also on her knees, behind and to the left of him, and her face wore a similar stricken look. She was lighted only by the pallid sky; her hair, slightly darker than the trees, coursed down her back and over her white shoulders. Her naked body, flushed blue like thin milk, seemed to glimmer faintly. She extended her arms to Narcissus who could not see her, and in her eyes there was such anguish, Claire could barely look at them. Again she was seeing her father's eyes, lost and naked. Averting her own gaze from Echo she walked closer to the canvas, and was struck by just how closely the two figures mirrored each other.

So, she thought, perhaps Echo is very like Narcissus, seeing, when she looks at him only her own reflection, her own desire for perfection. He is just a beautiful vessel to contain her longings, and that is why she cannot speak. And Narcissus resembles Echo, unable to see, mute in his failure. His true self is drowned at the pool's bottom – it is only his echo that remains, on the surface of the water.

Owen said, 'What do you think?'

Jolted out of her reverie, she paused. 'It does seem to be Moreno's brushwork. And Echo's face... It's so like the face

122

of his Saint Catherine, isn't it? And the light...'

'Yes,' Owen replied, 'Light as theatre. Similar to Velasquez, don't you think? And look—' He indicated the fine cracks which sprayed throughout the paint. 'The *craquelure* is extremely convincing, isn't it?'

Simon, behind them, asked, 'What do you mean by "convincing", Owen? How could someone fake a pattern of cracks?'

'My dear Simon,' said Owen, 'It's all too easy. You apply heat to a picture and the pigments splinter, or you tug a canvas across a table and the paint breaks into a web of cracks.'

Claire ventured, 'But often those kinds of cracks look too geometrical. In real *craquelure*, which takes many, many years to form, the fissures are much more random than the phoney kind, unless, of course, you are dealing with the work of a very skilled forger.'

'And indeed so many *are* very skilled,' sighed Owen. 'Some fakers manage to get their hands on authentic panels and canvases, which they paint over, so that when experts examine the work it seems genuinely old.'

'And some counterfeiters even make their pigments in the old-fashioned way,' Claire said, 'by brewing minerals and draw-ing the blood of flowers and so on, so that chemical analyses can't determine whether the paint is modern or centuries old.'

Simon came up next to them and draped his arm over Claire's shoulder. 'What if this picture is not a *modern* forgery, but not a Moreno, either?'

Owen smiled. 'You mean done by a contemporary of Moreno? Unlikely. Moreno was something of a maverick, you know, like his renegade pal Caravaggio. He never had much of a workshop, and his style was very distinctive.' He looked at

Claire. 'No, if this is a fake, it's a modern fake, but I have already asked an expert friend of mine from the Louvre to examine the canvas and pigments, without alerting anyone, of course, and he has determined that they are authentic. So now the final verdict is pretty much up to me, or should I say–' he touched Claire's arm – 'up to us.'

'Oh, no,' she demurred, genuinely alarmed. 'Don't flatter me! I'm not–'

Owen gave her an exaggeratedly severe look. 'Please don't be *modest*, Claire; I can't bear that. You are an intelligent and talented art historian, whose writing is not only fine, but blessedly unaffected. As far as I am concerned, your sense, right at this moment, of the painting, how you feel about it, is more valuable to me than a thousand pompous pronounce-ments by all the pseudo-experts on the globe. So no more modesty. Simply tell me, what your response, your *intuitive* response, is to the picture, right at this moment. Don't think too much; just tell me.'

She glanced around at Owen's hotel suite, done in a Louis XIV style, all curlicues and flocked wallpaper, with a number of low mahogany tables and scrolled couches. A fire burned in the large hearth, flushing the gilt designs on the chairs and ceiling with a ruddy light. Above the mantel there hung an incongruous reproduction of Rembrandt's 'The Jewish Bride', the couple gazing bashfully at each other.

Claire looked back at the 'Echo and Narcissus'. 'Well, I see such tremendous psychological depth in this picture. It's in their faces, a kind of grief and lostness. It seems clear that this painter understood the myth on that level, how it is really about the failure to love.' She looked at Owen. 'Do you know how some critics say that Moreno's pictures are so full of pathos that they're nearly masochistic? I've always disagreed. For instance, this painting depicts great sorrow, but not quite abasement. And the light along Narcissus's body and on their faces is marvellous; it reveals their spiritual and emotional truths, doesn't it? I think...' She spoke the last words slowly, 'I think it must be authentic,' and paused, as the implications – for her listeners and herself – became clear.

'Well, well,' said Owen, smiling softly, as though to himself. He touched her arm again. 'You and I are like-minded. I'd have hated to subject this poor canvas to all those experts who are so eager to use their bright machines, when it should be perfectly clear to any careful eye that this is a genuine Moreno. *Everything* looks so authentic, the crackle pattern, the brushwork, and of course the signature.'

Simon, who had withdrawn a little, now came up beside them again. 'All your art talk is reminding me of something. Once, this rich collector invited me to his Park Avenue apartment, to admire his paintings, especially this Velasquez portrait that he said he'd just bought, of the Infanta of Castille.'

Claire said, 'That little girl with her boiled-egg eyes and golden clothes.'

'Exactly. Anyway, I looked at my collector friend's picture and made the right noises, telling him how impressed I was and so forth, but for some reason he didn't seem satisfied with my reaction. It was weird, he just kept smiling and asking me to look at the painting again. So finally I stopped trying to flatter him and I simply stared at it for a while, without saying anything.'

'And?' asked Claire.

He laughed. 'I realised why he'd wanted me to just shut up and look at the painting. The more I looked, the less I saw.'

She grinned. 'While if it had been a real Velasquez it would have deepened under your gaze.'

'Yes; if it had been real it would have yielded up more complexity the longer I looked at it, but this painting, this so-called Velasquez, seemed to become more and more shallow. The kid's hands, I realised, were dead-looking, and the proportions of her face were all wrong. The whole composition collapsed before my eyes. It was my first lesson in fakery.'

'And this painting here?' asked Owen slowly. 'When you try to sound it...?'

Simon gazed long at the painting; then meditatively down at his own hands, discoloured from years of paint. When he looked up again he was smiling. 'When I sound this picture, I find unexpected depths. And, Owen, considering that it is so good, and all the materials are genuine as you say, can there be much doubt as to its authenticity?'

Owen went over to a drinks table, on which a cluster of bottles gleamed in the firelight, and poured out three more balloons of cognac. 'Honestly, I never had much doubt. And Claire's conclusions have confirmed my own.' He took a gulp of brandy, and grinned. 'At my advanced age, after such a long career of collecting and appraising and general pirateering, one develops a certain instinct. I don't mean to boast, but, really, sometimes it astonishes even me, this instinct of mine. Sometimes all I have to do is *glance* at a picture, and I know immediately whether it's a fake or not. And I am almost never wrong.' He tilted his head towards the glowing 'Echo and Narcissus,' on its easel in the corner. 'The minute I looked at this I knew it was a Moreno; I just knew it. Didn't you?' He smiled at Claire.

'I want it to be a Moreno,' she answered, smiling back, 'It's such a lovely painting, I *want* it to be.'

# Part Two

...I am this:
I am your moon,
shining without
a mouth.

I am the face
inside the lake.
I am the voice
out of the rock.
I am the ghost
of the music you lost.
And I am the cause
of this, who if
not I?

'Echo'
John O'Leary

# Chapter Thirteen

Over the next few days an extraordinary series of things happened.

Claire had always half-resisted doing her own work. Some perverse force in her would often dull her enthusiasm just as she was settling at her desk. But now something was changing. Her Caravaggio book seemed suddenly possible, felt possible. She believed in it. Walking home from Simon's loft the day after their dinner with Owen, she remembered a particular feeling she'd had as a small girl in the handball court at school, when other children's voices, slightly forlorn, had floated to her on the wet grey air. Why, she had actually given that feeling a name, a made-up name, *kina* or *krina*, something like that; she couldn't remember exactly, but the word had contained the grey sky, the hollow sound of handballs striking stone, the children's voices, a certain loneliness that was sometimes sweet. Now she wondered why her head was full of such insignificant but luminous memories, such old images? She couldn't say, but when she arrived back at her apartment they were transferred into a desire to write, not about those recollections of her early life, but her book, her Caravaggio book.

She had made herself a cup of coffee, and even its flavour was particularly delicious. She began to write a paragraph about how Caravaggio had captured light, harnessed it to transform the commonplace. But when she finally stopped, massaging her right shoulder, she realised that she had written six or seven paragraphs, nearly the whole introduction. It was almost evening.

She stood up and went over to the window, still wondering. Perhaps it was seeing the painting, and talking to Owen Kettlethorpe, that had inspired her. He had said last night that he would make a public announcement in a few weeks, in which he would reveal the existence of Moreno's astonishing painting. Smiling over his brandy glass, he had also promised that he would acknowledge Claire's help, describe how her observations had elucidated certain matters for him. There was no doubt that such a benediction, from so famous an art expert as Owen, would be a boon to her. Already his praise had strengthened her resolve. She would stop dithering, listlessly scribbling articles for *ArtDimension*. There was this book in her and she would write it.

It occurred to her that she might also have been inspired by two letters she had read today. The first was a photocopy of a letter written by Simon to a Columbia art history professor, in May 1987.

*Dear Louis,*

*Thank you for your encouragement last Tuesday. I am beginning to feel really rotten about some of my recent decisions. I mean, how I've sold out. Of course I know this is a cliché, the sensitive artist wringing his hands and complaining about how the corrupt world has soiled him, but I'm not complaining about the corrupt world; I'm thinking that I've deceived myself into believing that I have been developing as a painter when really something else, something pretty awful, has been going on. When I thought I was compelled by need, by passion, by the desire to get the vision right, I was lying to myself. I had a horror of losing my purchase on the New York art scene, of being thought of as old-fashioned, so I corrupted my own talent. Sometimes I did it consciously, really 'post-modern' and snide. Or else I convinced myself that I was actually painting from that deep place of need and vision, but I was lying. And I fear that everything I wanted to keep by this deception I am losing anyway, because I'm killing the only thing that matters.*

*Sorry for the melodrama. God rescue me from self-pity! Let me say it another way. I'm worried about my flight into abstraction. I've begun to suspect that a certain kind of abstract art can be dangerous, because it eliminates the human form. I know this has been said but I never really understood before. If you are just painting circles and panels and runnels of colour, if the human figure is no longer impli-cated in your work, you can cease to care. You've replaced humanity with an abstraction, so you can renounce political and social responsibility, as well as compassion, and even love. You're not involved in the human story any more, in the fact of faces and bodies, of sex, of grief and decay, of love. I also think it's somehow connected with the loss of meaning in our whole society. Imagine what Goya would have done with a zombie like Reagan! I know Goya was a court painter (we all have to be, to live) but he broke loose as well. A good deal of abstract art is like Republican politics, whitewashing away the pain.*

*The problem now is that I don't know how to get back. I keep thinking of moving to Ireland, my ancestral home. I remember my first glimpse of that extraordinary Irish country-side, from the window of a plane: small green fields, the silver curve of a river, a feeling of compactness and density under that rich sky, like an illustration in a children's story-book. It was instantly familiar to me, since I'd pictured the country so clearly from my Irish grandfather's stories. He had described stiles filigreed with lichen, a ruined keep in their neighbour's field, secret streams. And from the plane it looked so wonderfully different from America's raw land-scape, so much more* human, *a land lived on and worked for aeons, ancient yet intimate. I don't see why I can't go back, to live, to paint. Others have done it. And the painting there is still* sane, *still connected to history, to culture...*

The second letter was also from 1987, written by a man whom Claire had assumed was an architect.

*Dear Mr Brady,*

*Here is the answer to your question. Grecian temples are always supported by columns, regimental and stern. But above the columns is the lintel, which is a* liminal *place, a kind of threshold, if you will. Above the lintel the ornamentation is quite marvellous, as though the temple were*

*bursting into flower. The lintel is charged with conflict,
possibility, and tension. I do lament the fact that modern
architecture has abolished that place of promise above which
the temple flowers into a profusion of vines and blossoms.
Where are we without that source?*

*I am grateful for your letter and pleased that you enjoyed
my lecture, especially since the audience was largely hostile,
as you know. Incidentally, one sees another example of the
liminil, and the efflorescence above it, in Gothic rose windows...*

Claire was still looking out of her own window. Spring had
arrived in earnest; there was even a lace of watery green
leaves on the tree just outside her building. The stoops of the
houses across the street were thronged with children, gossiping Russian and Puerto Rican grandmothers all wearing
sacklike dresses and cool East Village kids in their ubiquitous
black with rings in their noses, and their hair twisted into
dreadlocks. Cars cruised along, music blaring from their open
windows.

Today, as she was leaving his loft, Simon had said, 'Isn't it
a little bit crazy, how you keep going back to the East Village
every day, and even last night, after we saw Owen? I think we
should talk about you moving in here sometime soon.'

She had gone to live with Jeremy for a while, in his apartment on Jane Street. And one hot summer night he had made
love to her there in a certain cold way he had, as though he
were contemptuous of her. And on this particular night his
coldness recalled something to her. She couldn't place the
memory at first – was it of her mother? When drink had
coarsened her into a blowsy creature, Claire had wrapped
herself in prim contempt of her, her only weapon. She hadn't

known, then, that self-abandon can take many forms, some of them creative and delightful. No, at that time, sex, boozing, gluttony, had all been one to her, all were pleasures that had gone rank, that had curdled into something dangerous, all realised in her mother's lewd drunkenness. But now with Jeremy *she* was her mother, lascivious, hungry, while he smiled contemptuously at her. And in that hot room on Jane Street, while she'd cried out in a kind of anguish of passion, a lust born of shame, it had never occurred to her that the disgust in his eyes might not be directed at her at all but against himself.

Simon must have seen her face change, because after making his suggestion he amended quickly, 'It's true, darling, we don't know each other well enough yet. But you might want to keep some clothes here, and a toothbrush, so that you can sleep over occasionally? It would make things simpler.'

Now the phone rang. It was Darby Holland, who was thinking of visiting Zoë, and wondered if Claire might come along. Claire had introduced them to each other, and Darby had immediately liked Zoë, just as Claire had been drawn to her, despite, or maybe because of, her wild and different life.

Darby was thirty-five, and lean as an El Greco. His bony face looked habitually mournful, and he often gave dolorous sighs while tugging at his black hair. But Claire had realised some time ago that this lugubrious manner of his was a kind of deception; he was actually rather happy by temperament, only he had probably decided at some point in his career that angst was a more useful attitude than optimism, since cynics and pessimists were allowed to say almost anything. So he'd learnt to conceal his cheeriness behind a show of melancholy, although this show convinced hardly anyone.

Claire agreed to meet him in Zoë's apartment. It was growing dark and she had switched on her kitsch lamps. She and Darby were doing coke at the coffee table, which was cluttered with a bowl of shrivelled grapes, a plate of desiccated cheese (on which Zoë was putting out her cigarettes), a used tea-bag, four dirty wine glasses, a crusted mascara wand, and the drowsing cat. Zoë was wearing a loose black dress and a golden necklace. Her yellow eyes looked smoky and gorgeous. 'Hey, baby,' she cried as Claire came in, 'this pal of mine Lloyd got himself some real smooth Colombian, and he gave me some. You come over here and help us out.'

'Hello, Pumpkinhead,' said Darby in his *Weltschmerz* way. Even drugs could not paint a smile on his gloomy face.

'My hair is *auburn*, not pumpkin-coloured,' Claire rebuked him, settling on the floor. Because of her mother's excesses she was usually wary of drink and drugs, especially coke which was so seductive with its twenty minutes of rapture before the fall. But today she couldn't resist, because there was such a turmoil within her, such conflicting feelings. She was full of a now-familiar love and yearning for Simon, and the work she'd done this afternoon had made her want to sing with happiness. But she was also anxious – the usual anxiety born of new love with all its uncertainties and dreams – coupled with an unease about her father, since she hadn't spoken to Cecily in a few days.

Darby passed her the straw and she drew the scorching powder into her nose. Immediately she was buoyed up as if on air.

'How's Willa?' she asked Darby. Willa was Darby's girl-friend, a ballet dancer.

'Gone,' he answered in a glum voice, like a bell tolling.

'*Dead?*' asked Zoë, wide-eyed.

'No, no. She's gone on tour, to Minnesota or something. She'll be back next month.' He looked at Claire. 'So how's it going, Pumpkinhead?'

It was the coke making her incautious, she knew, but she also knew that these two friends were loyal, and would not betray confidences. Or was the coke blurring her judgement about that, too?

Anyway, she pitched into a sprawling account of Owen Kettlethorpe and the painting, not revealing too much, she thought, saying only that she had met the renowned Mr Kettlethorpe and that he had asked her to look at this mysterious picture with him.

Darby dragged his hands excitedly through his hair. 'C'mon, Pumpkinhead, tell us more. *What* mysterious picture? Have you seen it? Stop being coy and give us that scoop. Remember, I helped you get that job with Brady in the first place.'

'Mr Holland,' Claire replied sternly, affecting a nineteenth-century manner, 'certainly you would never be so vulgar as to suggest that I am *obliged* to divulge everything about this matter, simply because you made the honourable gesture of recommending my services to Mr Brady?'

'Obliged? Obliged? Because I told Brady that you were bright and talented, because he was so impressed with your *ArtDimension* articles which I had given him that he decided to take you on as his assistant, because without my intervention you would never have met the eminent but very slippery Owen Kettlethorpe? Because I'm your best and oldest pal on earth? Of course I would never suggest that you were obliged!' It was obvious he was sky-high.

Claire grinned. 'All right. But you mustn't tell *anyone.* And I don't approve of your rapacious curiosity, Darby Holland.'

'Are you accusing me of not caring about *art*?'

They all burst into raucous, coke-jagged laughter.

Zoë said, 'Before you start talking I will serve us some Pernod.'

She disappeared into the kitchen and returned presently with three glasses of *pastis* and a jug of water. They all drank while Zoë prepared three more ribbons of coke on the table; after they'd each had a blast she said to Darby, 'I am glad Claire is telling us about this painting and that man, Owen Kettlesomething. And, incidentally, she has also told me that she and her new boss –'

'Zoë.'

Zoë placed a hand over her mouth and giggled. 'Sorry, baby. I guess I am just a little high.'

Darby threw Claire a wry look. 'Surprise, surprise.'

'What's that supposed to mean?' she asked brusquely.

He gave one of his disconsolate sighs. 'You're very romantic, Pumpkinhead, and Simon is a romantic figure. So I'm not surprised that you got involved with him. He's also full of secrets.'

'Secrets?'

'His marriage, the real story. He never talks about it. I only met the wife once, and she seemed pretty troubled. Wouldn't talk, and kept tilting her head down the whole time, as if she wanted her hair to drop forward and conceal her face, which it did do, so I have no real picture of what she looked like. I think she was chronically depressed or something. Anyway, you probably know a lot more about Simon's personal life than I do, since you've been perusing his epistles, as you would say.'

'I haven't spoken to him much about his marriage,' said Claire irritably. 'And I know I'm too romantic, which is why I'm being careful now. And I don't want to talk about this any more.'

Darby grinned. 'All right. Let's talk about the painting instead.'

So Claire told them about Claude Caron, and about seeing the 'Echo' the previous night in Owen's hotel suite. 'I was really impressed with that painting,' she sighed, 'and I do think it has the authority of the genuine.'

She looked at Darby, who was pouring more water into his Pernod. He was nearly ugly with his rough hair and saturnine face, but his intelligence, and the dry sense of humour which tempered his glumness despite himself, always made him look lovely to her. She went on, 'A lot of art seems ungenerous and self-absorbed these days. And books, too. What has happened to the social novel, that really daring kind, where people's individual lives and their whole culture are interwoven? One seldom sees amplitude like that any more, in any of the arts.'

'You believe artists have chosen not to care?' asked Darby.

Remembering Simon's letter to the Columbia art historian, she answered, 'I think they've chosen not to feel. And then I see this painting, this "Echo and Narcissus", and it expresses the narcissistic affliction of our age: that boy looking up from his reflection with a stricken face, and behind him the girl... The pain is *in the light*.'

Zoë asked, 'How much money would your friend Mr Kettlesomething make from selling a painting like that, a real Old Master?'

Claire laughed. 'A great deal. In this instance he's a sort of broker, I suppose, selling the "Echo" to a private collector on behalf of the Caron family. But I'm sure there's a lot of money involved.'

Just then the phone rang. When Zoë came back she was grinning. 'Baby, speaking of money, I have a business proposition to make to you.'

Claire and Darby looked at each other. 'What kind of proposition?' Claire asked warily.

Zoë returned to the floor, arranging her dress so that it flowed becomingly around her. Claire was feeling herself slump as the coke waned in her, but she thought it would be tactless to ask Zoë to chop up some more. 'What kind of proposition?' she repeated.

Zoë lit a cigarette. 'You know, some of my clients, they just want to be seen with a pretty girl, to impress people. They are small town businessmen on the loose in the big city, and their dream is to take a *soignée* lady out to dinner. Did you know that I have never been to bed even one single time with some of my regular clients?' She emptied more coke onto the table. 'So, anyway, this regular client of mine, Andrew, is in town tonight from Detroit for some convention. And he is with a friend. And this friend would like a dinner companion.'

'Zoë...'

Zoë narrowed her already narrow, golden eyes. 'How much money did you say you are making at this painter's?'

'Fifteen an hour.'

'Well, the man who I am discussing would like to give you two hundred dollars. Two hundred, *for eating dinner*. Nothing else, honey, I promise.'

'I can't believe that this businessman – I presume he's in

the car business since he lives in Detroit – is willing to deprive himself of two hundred dollars for the privilege of buying me a meal.'

Zoë polished off her Pernod. 'My customer's friend, Richard, doesn't want to be lonely this evening. He just wants the company of a pleasant woman, who he can wine and dine a little, so he's not all by himself. And Andrew would like to oblige this man for business reasons. That's the entire story. Plus you would be doing me a favour. If I please Andrew, it's good business for me. And he's a nice man, baby, with a nice friend. Nothing sordid.'

Claire sighed. 'You're sure it's just for dinner?' Half of her couldn't believe she was considering this; never before had she ventured into Zoë's real world, a world of murmured assignations, of overfed businessmen drinking Martinis in hotel lounges, of glamorous parties and dangerous games, of room after room and man after man, some of them nice, maybe, and interesting, TV producers and diplomats, and others perhaps not so nice. Claire had never wanted to know too much about it all. But now there was this recklessness in her, which might be merely a coke-rashness, or perhaps something else, something deeper; she couldn't say.

'Do you think I'm crazy?' she asked Darby. Zoë had gone into the bedroom to look for a dress that Claire might borrow.

He stared down at the begrimed coffee table. 'Listen, Pumpkinhead, something about you has always been drawn to the lowlife.'

Startled, she nearly protested, until she remembered her affection for Emory the junkie and, of course, her friendship with Zoë herself.

Darby continued, 'On the other hand, you're so naïve and

140

almost otherworldly, as though you'd never experienced anything dark, anything squalid, in your whole life. It's like your name, *Claire* for the naïve side of you, that likes to live only in the light and talk romantically about paintings, and *Browne* for the dark side, which is drawn to bohemia and likes to get plastered and stoned and live a little bit dangerously.' Finally he looked at her. 'When I worry about you it's because the two sides are not always connected. Your lowlife side and your idealism don't *meet*. Which means that in some ways you're a stranger to yourself; you don't always know what you're doing.'

Claire was silent. As though afraid he'd spoken too bluntly, Darby squeezed her arm. 'I'm not saying you shouldn't go out with Zoë tonight. Just don't let anything get out of hand.' He gave his morose laugh. 'Anyway, two hundred dollars is two hundred dollars. And this *is* the era of the fast buck, in the republic of the greenback, *n'est-ce pas?*'

\* \* \*

Zoë dressed Claire in a short, forest-green silk dress and black stockings. She also poured a healthy amount of the cocaine into a vial so that she and Claire could snort some in the restaurant toilet.

Darby said, 'Well, have fun. I'm going home. I've had enough drugs and debauchery for one evening. Remember what I told you, Pumpkinhead.'

'I'll try to,' she assured him, smiling nervously.

# Chapter Fourteen

The restaurant was a French bistro in the old-fashioned New York style; no camp downtown glamour, just a number of plain tables in a rosy room in the west Fifties, full of soberly dressed people eating plates of decent food and drinking decent wine. It was the kind of place Claire's parents had taken her to when she was a child, before or after the theatre. She had been dazzled, then, by the waiters, their legs aproned in white, and by the exotic things to eat: pâté, coquilles Saint Jacques, escargots.

Zoë had done Claire's hair, piling it up loosely on her head. They both wore golden earrings and necklaces, and had painted their mouths crimson.

Zoë's Andrew looked about Simon's age, forty-five or so.

He was a hearty, slightly rotund, dull man whose ruddy cheeks reminded Claire of Hals' Laughing Cavalier. She realised that she rather liked her fellow, Richard, who seemed remarkable for his total ordinariness. He was thinner than Andrew, with thin grey hair and a shy, courtly manner – he was considerate of Claire in an old-fashioned gentlemanly way – decorous rather than dashing.

In the manner of out-of-town businessmen living it up in the Big Apple, the men ordered whiskey sours. 'Would you like one too?' asked Andrew.

Claire said, 'I would like a Campari, please.'

Richard looked baffled. 'I don't think I've ever seen that drink.'

Claire smiled at him. 'It is a lovely red colour.'

'So is your hair,' he murmured; then glanced shyly down. Zoë asked for a Martini.

The conversation after that was so stilted and charged with silences that Claire and Zoë might have been boarding school girls out with their fathers on parents' day. The men chose serious platters: shrimp cocktail; then 'surf and turf', gross steaks garlanded with seafood; and they drank whiskey sours the whole time. But they were impressed when Claire and Zoë selected more subtle dishes: asparagus with hollandaise sauce; grilled salmon; and glasses of white wine. Claire herself was impressed when the conversation, after some desperate attempts to locate common ground, collapsed finally onto sports, and Zoë all of a sudden displayed an encyclopaedic knowledge of the exploits of the Detroit Tigers. As far as Claire knew, Zoë had never been to any kind of ball game in her life, but here she was spouting lore and statistics like a sportswriter. Or like a Grecian *hetira*, more courtesan than prostitute, knowledgeable and wise in myriad ways.

Anyway, she certainly put Andrew and Richard at their ease, and by the time the after-dinner drinks arrived, they were both beaming. Zoë sipping a Crème de Menthe, placed her hand on Andrew's arm, and while he went on discussing some retired pitcher who 'threw heat like you wouldn't believe'. Slowly, she moved her scarlet-manicured fingers up his sleeve, and buried them in his hair. He stopped talking and half closed his eyes, like a cat. Zoë whispered something in his ear, and they both stood up.

"Bye, honey,' said Zoë. Andrew pointed a plump finger at Claire and Richard. 'Now you two kids have fun, do you hear?' Zoë took his arm and tilted her beautiful face up to his.

After they'd gone Richard said awkwardly, 'Well, would you like another brandy?'

She actually wanted to go home, especially since she and Zoë had done the last of the coke in the Ladies, and she was beginning to come down. But she thought that it would be ungracious to leave too hastily; after all, she would be receiving two hundred dollars plus dinner from this man. 'Yes. That would be very nice. Thank you.'

He examined his hands on the table. He had a long face with mild grey eyes and a surprisingly full, mobile mouth – but it said nothing. Growing desperate in the thickening silence she blundered, 'Did you know, did I tell you, I'm an art historian?'

'Really?' He looked at her politely.

'Yes. I - I study pictures.'

'That must be very nice.'

'Yes.'

They drank nervously from their glasses. Finally, he said,

'Would you like to see some pictures of my family?'

'I'd like that very much.'

He produced his wallet. 'I'm sentimental, I guess, carrying these around.'

'It's touching that you do.'

'This is Cal, my boy. He's at Ann Arbor.'

'That's a very good university.'

'And here I am with my daughter, Hannah, when she was twelve. She died last year. She was only sixteen.'

'Oh,' breathed Claire, truly distressed, 'I'm so sorry.'

'Cancer. There was a drug that they said might save her, but it wasn't FDA approved, so we had to go down to Mexico and smuggle it into the country. And then it didn't do her any good, anyway.'

'How terrible. And only last year.'

He looked back down at the table. His sparse grey hair, the childlike curve of his ear, and the slightly raw-looking skin beneath it, as though his collars irritated him, were moving her to an almost unbearable pity.

He said gruffly, 'I know that you're not a - a professional, like your friend. Andy told me. And I'm glad, you know. All I wanted was someone nice, someone like you, to talk with.' He paused. 'Would you like to see a picture of my wife?'

'Please.'

It was not a good photograph, the face blurred, the background too dark. She had curly fair hair, and was wearing a pink blouse. 'She's pretty,' said Claire.

'Well, she used to be. She's getting on, you know. I guess I am too.'

Claire wondered if it was something about business and life in America's vast middle west, that persuaded a man to

145

believe he and his wife were old at forty-five. No, probably it
was the tragedy; there is no worse blow, perhaps, than the
death of one's child. She imagined them staring at each other
in a suburban house, growing hollow-cheeked before each
other's eyes, the sap draining out of them.

As if reading her mind, he continued, 'Our lives seem to be
over in that department, if you know what I mean. But we still
like each other.'

The waiter appeared with their bill. 'Thank you,' said
Claire. Richard returned his wallet to his pocket. 'Why don't
you walk me back to my hotel? Andy and I are at the Hilton,
just down the street. And then I'll give you some money for a
taxi.'

'Oh, no...'

'I insist. New York isn't safe at night for a pretty young
woman.'

Sixth Avenue blazed with the glistering lights of cars, and
the glow of cafés and hotels. This was the New York she often
forgot about, full of sumptuous shops, horse-drawn cabs, and
tourists in their finery. She allowed Richard to take her hand.

But at the entrance to the hotel, among the taxis, limou-
sines, and liveried porters, he suddenly drew her close in a
kiss, and in a kind of dream she found herself accepting it. He
had pressed the entire length of his body against hers, and his
hands moved heavily up and down her back; he gave a kind of
groan, deep in his throat. She tried to break away.

He said, 'I'm sorry. I didn't mean... I'm going back home
tomorrow, you see, and I'll be lonely tonight. I thought maybe
you'd like to come up to my room, just for a little while. We
could just talk, if you'd like, or I could order you up some
Campari. Whatever you'd like. I have more photographs of

my daughter in the room. I loved her very much. I'd like to be able to feel love again.'

Above them was the hotel, a honeycomb of lighted windows, in which his rubicund friend and Zoë were probably embracing at this very moment, in a big bed with tousled sheets, two sticky brandy glasses on the floor beside them, and the television switched soundlessly on to a porn channel. '*Not a professional*,' he'd said, but she was here with him now. And he was drawing his wallet out of his coat again and pressing two one hundred dollar bills into her hand.

She thought about what would happen if she accepted his invitation, came up with him. Not much, she decided, not much, despite his ardour of a moment before. He would revert to his favourite at-home drink, beer probably, or bourbon, and grow thoughtful, or sentimental, or lachrymose, the tears for his daughter oozing out of those wan eyes. And finally he would lay his head on her breast, murmuring his daughter's name, and she would loosen his tie, take off his shoes, settle him into bed, and slip away, with a final, light kiss on the cheek.

Suddenly, and for the first time, she was truly, even deeply, enticed by Zoë's life, or a variation of it. Of course her own services would be different. She could even imagine the ad she might place in certain magazines, under Escort Services: *Petite redhead, well-spoken and intelligent, available for dinner, conversation, and mild ministrations, especially to the hurt, the lonely, the heartsick...*

How nice it would be to ease a man's pain for a time, to diminish her own pain through that gift, to banish her own loneliness for a night without becoming entangled in the thickets of herself, in fact to lose herself, transform herself into someone else, someone glamorous, a stranger, free from familiar weaknesses, as Zoë did. Opulent hotels, fine restaurants, herself rendered desirable through clothes and makeup: it would be a dream...

Abruptly, she roused herself, shaking her head.

Jesus, what had she been thinking! What did she think she was up to? She was nearly thirty years old and had not yet begun to live. Dreams and dust and fatuous fantasies! If she were weak and helpless, or truly desperate, she might consider work as a courtesan or concubine, but she was talented and healthy, with books to write, and Simon, in whom she wanted to believe. *What was she doing here?* She felt like thrusting the money back at Richard, and hurrying away, her head bowed.

But when she looked at his face she realised what that refusal would mean to him. How would he feel, if she disdained his attentions *and* his money, if she made him return alone into that vulgar hotel, the two bills crumpled in his hand, while Andrew and Zoë fucked the night away next door?

Richard was smiling sadly. She kissed his dry cheek. 'Thank you,' she said, 'I'll take this money, though I don't think I really deserve it. You are a nice man and I'm sorry I can't stay with you; maybe some other time. It was very kind of you to take me out to dinner.'

'The taxi,' he said, gesturing feebly. 'Won't you let me call you one, and give you some more money?'

'No,' she answered, 'No, thank you. I'd like to walk a little. I usually enter into a kind of dream, walking. And please don't worry about me. I've lived in this town all my life.'

She was really crashing now; her hands had begun to tremble, and a gloom was lapping at the corners of her consciousness, like an oily sea. No wonder, after all that coke and alcohol. She wanted to walk it off, and sleep. 'Good bye, Richard,' she said, and turned away before he could speak.

But as she was walking along Sixth Avenue in the after-theatre crush, she looked behind her and saw him there, at the entrance to the Hilton, a still, grey figure, gazing after her. She raised an arm, and so did he, and they stood like that for a second.

# Chapter Fifteen

That same night Simon had gone out to dinner in Little Italy with his friend Louise Vye, a painter, and her droll accountant husband. The husband was as fat as Louise was lean, and he made excited, expansive gestures the whole time, spattering sauce all over his cardigan. Louise, on the other hand, was her usual tranquil self, and in the din of that garish Italian restaurant she had smiled and talked in her measured way, crumbling some bread in her fingers while she told Simon about Luke Reilly's new foray into sculpture, consisting of erotic statues of himself and his wife made from peppers, cucumbers, tomatoes, and parsnips. Simon had managed not to choke on his *insalata caprese*.

When he got home the phone was ringing. He thought it might be Owen, because Owen never slept, but it was Claire.

An urgency about her manner told him that she'd been trying to phone for a while. And he could also tell, by something bleared and furry about her voice, that she was either drunk or stoned.

'Simon?' she quavered, 'I was doing a lot of coke tonight with Darby Holland and my friend Zoë, and then we went out to dinner and drank all this wine and brandy, and now I'm feeling awful – that bleak, *scourged* feeling. I would like to come over. Would that be all right?'

'Of course, darling. I'm feeling lonely myself. Take a taxi, though. It's too late for walking.'

When she arrived he immediately noticed that she was wearing make-up. He'd never seen her face made-up before, and it was slightly unnerving. She looked closer to her age, and even siren-like, with a reddened mouth and some black stuff around her eyes. She'd also put her hair up, and the dress she was wearing, a short, filmy, emerald thing, was uncharacteristically sexy. But when she came up to embrace him he saw that the paint on her mouth and cheeks was smudged, and her body shuddered in his arms. Her hair smelled like a bar.

Silently he brought her into the bathroom, where clumsily, gently, he took the pins out of her hair, which, surprisingly, had been lacquered with spray; then he eased her clothes off, and turned on the shower, coming in with her to give her a shampoo. She was docile as a child, and he, soaping her body, felt no desire, only a deep tenderness. As he wrapped her in a towel and brought her to bed she began to mumble in a way that was nearly incomprehensible.

'Oh, Simon,' she groaned, 'I keep thinking about my uncle Isaac, the day he died. There was a window in his apartment, thick and dull-green like bottle glass. Rachel didn't know he was dead, he had died in the hospital. She came to the door of the apartment, and the moment she saw my father her mouth opened in a big black "O", and my father pressed my face against his coat so that I wouldn't have to see her stricken face, but I *did* see it. And then this man I met tonight, he'd had to pirate some illegal drug in from Mexico but his daughter died anyway...'

Simon combed out her long hair. She was babbling, 'Carlos Moreno... That's like my own name, did you know? Moreno means brown, in Spanish.' He laid her head on the pillow. She clutched at his hand. 'My own name, Claire Browne. It means clarity and murk, it means light and dark- ness. *Claire Obscure. Chiaroscuro.* Moreno. Darkness. The world is so full of murk and rage and pain and darkness...' She moved her head restively. 'I look for the light...'

Rhythmically he stroked her brow, smoothing back the damp hair. Her lashes fluttered. She murmured, 'Light doesn't mean the absence of darkness. It is darkness *illuminated*, isn't it? There can be no light without darkness, after all, without a darkness to kindle. But what is light, Simon? Where is it?' She sighed, 'In work, I think. And love.' She gave a weary laugh. 'Though we are living in a time without God, of course. People don't believe in a redeemer anymore, do they? But there is still love.' She sighed again. 'How sentimental that sounds, these days.'

He drew the bedclothes up to her chin. What had happened to her tonight, with Darby and this exotic friend of hers? And who was this man she had mentioned, whose daughter had died? Simon was surprised to feel a tremor of jealousy. Claire squirmed under the sheets, and began to talk again, with an exhausted, febrile eloquence. 'Simon, don't you think that most people are too bitter, these days? Their loss of faith has soured them. They don't believe in miracles anymore. When I look at the old paintings, of saints with their emblems, and angels and Madonnas and Christ in his torment, how strange it is, to think that all those things were alive to people once, they were real, they meant something, they weren't just the icon-ography of a dead age. But now we believe that everything is finite and fragile, nothing abides, not even love can save us.' Again she clutched his hand. 'We are so cool in this age, so without heat; we let ourselves down if we *feel*. But love *can* save us, it *does* exist. The knowledge of someone else, a knowledge that can make us *responsible* for ourselves. The loss of faith doesn't have to mean the loss of human love, does it? Despite Jeremy, and my father...'

She closed her eyes, but kept talking. '*Chiaroscuro*... Rembrandt knew. That secret light, without any external source, that *radiance* in his face, in the late self portraits. And the backgrounds deepening, more and more darkness, until the only light on the canvas is that inward glow, a spirit-light...' She opened her eyes suddenly, and smiled up at him. 'Simon, I hate to destroy your romantic notion, but I'm afraid Rembrandt wasn't always poor and struggling. He had *many* wealthy patrons and patronesses, and made an awful lot of money. But poor or rich, he persisted in his vision, till light overcame darkness.' She released his hand, turned over on her side, and fell instantly asleep.

Simon put on his dressing gown, and went out past his studio into the living room. He wondered again what had happened to her, tonight? That raw, hectic gabbling, some of it pitching into incoherence, but other times making rather a lot of sense, in a weird way. And the sexy clothes and make-up. There was so much he still didn't know about her life, but he did love her.

It was simple, really. She belonged to him, not in the way of a possession, but as the one implicated in his life, the one he recognised with his own self, in his very guts. Her eagerness, her earnest way of talking, how she remembered people by their cheekbones or the colour of their eyes, how she sometimes scowled down at her plate while eating, her intelligence, her anxieties born of some early pain he still could not fathom. He recognised these things. But of course all definitions of love were reductive. He could maintain that he loved her for the reasons he'd just defined to himself, but if, for instance, her face were somehow to lose its particular earnest look, he would not love her less. And he had felt this way about her the minute she walked into his loft that very first day, he could not say how, or why. It just was.

\* \* \*

That evening, before going out with Louise Vye, he had ferreted among the papers Claire was organising for him, so as to remove from them anything that might disturb her. He had remembered a number of love letters he'd received during the last months of his marriage and afterwards, when he'd fallen with depressing regularity into the arms of many women, and he hadn't wanted Claire to stumble on them. Now he opened the drawer where he'd placed all those *billets doux*, and brought them to the sofa.

Here they were, the silt of his recent past. He would not be able to sleep tonight so he might as well look over them and reflect, especially since this deep dreaming hour, silent even in SoHo, was probably a good time for reflection.

Some of the letters were sweet, written by women he had genuinely liked, although none of those women had been *real* to him. It was not their fault; how could they be real, when he'd known them so glancingly? They had been encounters more than relationships, lively girls who had briefly distracted him from the anguish of his collapsing marriage, whose appetite for life had served as an antidote to Olivia's growing despair, whose conversation had delighted him and whose bodies had often been lovely. He had met them only at special times, islanded from the dailiness of life, fugitive meetings for love-making, for holidays when they could arrange to get away, for passionate talks in obscure restaurants. They had been dream-creatures, those women, as he must also have been a dream to them, a famous artist but wounded in love, an attentive lover who brought them out to glamorous parties and introduced them to glamorous people. And when he was still married there had also been the thrill of the illicit, the charm of furtive embraces in hotel rooms or strange apartments. And of course some of the women had been unhappily married themselves...

Well, Simon thought, that explained the nice women, the pleasant affairs. But what of the others? He was fingering four letters bound with a red ribbon, all written in 1984 by a woman called Juliette Clarissa Marquand, a most unlikely name, but suited to Juliette, who had been gushing, theatrical, and self-absorbed. He opened the topmost letter:

*My glorious Simon,*

*Will you ever forget the night I threw you down on the old table in my kitchen and kissed you passionately with Matthew asleep just next door? Wasn't it daring of me? I'd never known I could be so fierce and brave. Afterwards when I looked in the mirror my face was glowing and beautiful. And it's all thanks to you, dear Simon. You saw I had an artistic temperament, darling!*

Wincing, he read the letter directly underneath:

*Dear, dear Simon,*

*The garden at my country house is blooming and I am relaxing in the hammock, drinking this awful wine that smells like turpentine. But of course I don't mind, since that smell recalls to me your studio and our marvellous talks there. Darling, I am confident that the deep connection between us will endure forever, and that I am your inspiration, as you are mine. How do I know this, even though you have stopped answering my phone calls and letters? I had a dream last night...*

Simon looked out the dark window, letting this letter flutter to the floor. Why, she was mad, he thought, I was just a cup she could pour her dreams into. He tried to conjure up a picture of Juliette but could barely recall her face. Had she been dark, fair, tall, short? He supposed he had been drawn to her because of her unabashed desire for him, which had flattered his vanity, especially since all his recent efforts to leaven Olivia's heavyheartedness had failed so miserably: surely he wasn't a complete failure if he could still attract such an alluring woman?

But where had he met Juliette? Ah, yes, she had come here one night with a photographer acquaintance of his, and, yes, now that he had placed their first meeting he could picture her more clearly, her extraordinary hair, long, black, and undulating. The evening she'd first come here, talking to him in her fey manner, she had twirled a tendril of that hair round and round her finger, mesmerising him. The photographer, Matthew Something-or-other, hadn't really minded her flirtation with Simon, nor their ensuing affair. In fact he'd told Simon one day that he could understand why a lot of men were attracted to Juliette, since she had 'muse quality', but then he had gone on to say that she was arch and histrionic and could get on people's nerves after a while, an observation with which Simon had had to agree.

He stood up and dragged on a cigarette, walking from window to sofa. He didn't want to read the other love letters, but for some reason felt obliged to do so. Settling down again he unearthed another packet, this one from a nice young woman called Kate who had lived in Westchester and with whom he'd had what he privately called a 'white' affair, meaning that it had been curiously chaste – affectionate, but not in the least passionate. He'd met this Kate when he was weakened after the ordeal of his divorce, half-convinced that Olivia's glooms had been his fault. Also, at that time, his career was already wobbling off-centre. The reviews were not what they had been, and the eighties were making themselves felt, a sulphur-stink in the political and artistic air.

Kate had been an art student, a warm-hearted girl whom he could not love, but whom he did like considerably. Her physical type was familiar to him from his early life in New England: that big-boned, healthy, Anglo-Saxon type, appealing if slightly porcine, all fair hair and ruddy cheeks and bright eyes. In a sad way she had been what he needed then, this robust, practical young woman who would thump him on the back and suggest they go out for a Chinese meal or to see a Woody Allen movie whenever he was feeling down. She was more like a pal or a kindly younger sister than a lover, although at first they had exchanged desultory caresses. But after a while even such light kisses and ministrations had begun to feel stilted to him, a meaningless duty, and when he ceased to offer them Kate did not object, which encouraged him to conclude that she must also prefer their chaste palship to anything more fleshly. They still slept together, cuddling like puppies, or bolstering themselves up on the pillows to eat childish things like brownies or popcorn while looking at television, but lovemaking was no longer even the remotest issue between them and, pathetically he supposed, he didn't even miss it.

But then things had gone wrong. Simon, reading her letters, tried to understand exactly when, and why. Perhaps the falseness, the plunging back into a kind of sexless adolescence implicit in their relationship, had begun at some point to tug at her, to make her uneasy. After all, she was a healthy woman with, he assumed, natural appetites. Also there was the matter of her silliness. Kate had always been a little bit silly, but over time her letters to him became increasingly giddy, childish, gauche, and with a new stridency in them, a teasing element that bordered on hostility. Finally, six months or so into their odd affair, she wrote him an abrupt postcard declaring that she had met a young man, 'a more suitable partner for me, closer to my age, and full of energy...' and that she and this fellow were moving to California.

Simon walked into the kitchen and looked at the clock. It was three in the morning, but still he couldn't sleep. He was wondering if these love affairs, these Juliettes and Kates, were connected in some essential way to his loss of himself, the loss of his artistic bearings. He thought also that it was ironical how his deepening loneliness over the years had reduced his expectations, so that the hungrier he was, the more meagrely he was fed; the more he needed love, the more he was inclined to settle for less than love, for someone juvenile like Kate, or fey and narcissistic like Juliette. Until Claire...

Again he returned to the sofa, and glanced through some of the other letters. With an uncharacteristic orderliness he had kept the models together. Models and painters, that enduring cliché—! He smiled to himself, reflecting that painting and sculpture, the most tactile of all the arts, had given a great many artists a great many excuses over the centuries to concentrate on the flesh in more ways than one.

He himself had always reacted to beauty in a way he presumed was unconventional. Fashion models, for example, had never moved him, with their attenuated limbs and vacuous, chameleon faces. When he was still doing the figure, and beginning to have his first early success, his model had been a Latin American woman with vast olive-green eyes in a harsh dark face. She'd had a crooked nose, and brown hair that fell in two straight panels down her sallow cheeks. Had she been ugly or beautiful? He hadn't known, still didn't know, or care: she had excited him, inspired him, that face with its sharp angles, the expanse of purplish skin above and beneath her eyes, the cords in her throat, her tough arms, cabled as a man's, her tiny breasts with their cinnamon-coloured nipples.

He and this particular model hadn't had an affair; those had come later, and not, he was certain, only as a result of the headiness of fame, of success and money. He truly believed

159

that he could have, would have resisted the models, despite their loveliness and the intimacy of his work with them, if only his marriage had been happier, if only it had offered even a modicum of sustenance. But while his career flourished Olivia began to grow morose and tearful, to withdraw from him sexually, to envy him his success while neglecting her own work, to break down. She refused to model for him any more or to let him model for her, refused to be encouraged in her own efforts, refused the consolations of love, would burst out crying the moment he tried to kiss her or even stroke her hair. And he had needed her for anchorage in this new, shrill, pseudo *demi-monde* of hype and big bucks, needed her for love in the loveless Big Apple, needed her to soothe him when he feared it was all a dream, when he grew convinced that he was really just another phoney and tomorrow they'd realise their mistake and throw him out of their fancy galleries.

But she withdrew when he needed her, and so he became what he had feared; a womanising artist who took an infantile delight in his prowess, who seduced models in his studio, whose picture appeared in the society pages with pretty girls on his arm. Oh, it was a sad story, Olivia sickening, growing paler and paler before his eyes like a photograph blanching in harsh sunlight, and then her retreat into hospitals and clinics, and his own frantic plunge into casual sex, especially after the divorce. And in the meantime the curious, erratic skyrocket of his career, his dread that it would plummet, that he would be left behind, which convinced him that he must move towards abstraction. Blunder after blunder...

He went quietly to look in on Claire. She was still sleeping deeply, her hair spread out on the pillow. He returned to the kitchen and poured himself a whiskey. Who *had* she been with earlier? Some mysterious man whose daughter had died. And hadn't she also mentioned Darby? Gloomy-faced Darby! Was it possible...? Again, jealousy curdled in him like bad food. But then, slurping at his whiskey, he chastened himself for entertaining such adolescent worries. Darby was her old friend, and anyway she'd come here, to him, for comfort.

His own peccadilloes were more the point. Bringing his glass back to the sofa he lightly touched all the packets of letters. Considering them made him feel slightly ashamed. He had been, in those days, so immature, a gluttonous child let loose in a pastry shop. He'd gobbled up all the sweetmeats with very little discrimination: Once, Olivia had accused him of behaving like a king, gazing down from his throne at his subjects and choosing the ones who pleased him. As though all those women had had no active, urgent lives of their own, as though they'd been merely the embodiments of his fantasies, as though their sole purpose in life had been to amuse him, as though they'd been passive, weak, grateful for his largesse. She'd been right, he realised, looking again at the letters, Olivia had been right.

And now, finally, he was coming close to answering his own question. There *was* a connection between his numerous affairs, the use of his bed as a trampoline, and the loss of his balance as an artist. The answer was simple: in those days he had ceased to care, had ceased, nearly, to feel. Doing coke with a couple of girls in their West Village studio and then sleeping with them both, painting a colour-field picture, fucking Juliette in her country house with poor old Matthew asleep in the next room, painting a little white-on-white number, sleeping with a photographer called Bronwen who'd venomously spilled the beans to Olivia, experimenting with

161

photo-realism: it had all been the same thing, and none of it had mattered very much, the bodies as indistinguishable in colour and form as his canvases.

Lighting another cigarette, he walked again to the living room window. A lamp burned behind one of the curtains across the street. Who lived inside that window? Another whiskey-drinking insomniac? A young boy or girl whooping it up in SoHo on Daddy's money? An old Italian couple who had withstood the onslaught of gentrification and kept their little flat despite the encroachment of *artistes* like himself?

His mind circled and dipped. What had Claire said about Rembrandt? The golden radiance in his old face, that light. 'Rich or poor,' she had said, 'he persisted in his vision...' She had also talked about love. Now he dared ask himself: through *his* love for Claire, and hers for him, might his own vision, so dimmed, be rekindled? Already, now, he was beginning to paint as he'd used to in the old days, in a state of joy and dread, in love with the textures and colours of things, a saffron-coloured dress, the tension of an extended arm, perhaps a face... It was years since he'd painted in that crazy wonderful state!

When he'd stumbled into Claire at Ted Rubenstein's party, she was standing with her forehead pressed against the window, and now he did the same, touching his hot brow to the chill glass. In the beginning there were things he had said automatically to her, to woo her: 'I like your face; maybe you will model for me..'. Arrogant gloating things, the famous painter sure of his power. But what had astonished him, taken him by surprise, was that they were true, all those things he'd said; he had meant them, every word.

And now what would he do, now that he was in this

pickle? He had thought it wouldn't matter, that one day he would simply tell her what he and Owen had done, and they would have a nice chuckle over it... Abruptly he crushed out his cigarette, and strode impatiently back to the sofa to tidy away the love letters.

Deceit, delusions, narcissism! He glanced at the pages, at Juliette's curlicues, Kate's childlike scrawl, Bronwen's neat paragraphs. Then, after placing all of them back in their drawer, he walked softly into the bedroom, threw off his dressing gown, and settled gingerly into bed beside Claire.

She was lying on her back, her mouth slightly open, one arm flung out on the pillow. At the moment she was no sleeping beauty; she was snoring lightly, and a ribbon of drool extended from her mouth to her ear. He drew down the bedclothes, and looked at her naked body. Something that had always delighted him about it was its secret lushness. Clothed, she seemed nearly frail, but actually her breasts were full, her hips rounded. He appled one breast, then moved his hand down over her stomach to the bone of her hip, then along her thigh to the curve of her knee. It was true that he would like to paint her. She was herself, and lovely to him. He covered her again, and lay down next to her to sleep as the dawn came in.

# Chapter Sixteen

Next morning, Claire felt ashamed, at first. She had come to Simon like a mendicant the night before, raw with need, extending her arms to him in the ancient gesture of appeal. What nonsense did I babble, she wondered now, what desperation did I expose, what hunger opened in me for him to be alarmed by?

'I list – sorry – lost my composure,' she tried, at breakfast. She was nearly dizzy with dismay.

He gave a tired smile. 'Yes, one could say that you were without repose, last night. Until you collapsed, of course, snoring.'

'Oh, Simon, did I *snore*?'

'Thunderously. Here, have some more coffee.'

So he had seen her at her worst, after an excess of drugs and booze and strange behaviour. And he had not turned from her.

Yet she was still too ashamed to tell him the details of her sybaritic evening with Zoë. Darby had divined a truth about her: she was afraid of the darkness of her feelings, which meant that she was sometimes at their mercy, and would continue to be so, unless she examined her own unreconciled desires. But she was still too cowardly, so that when Simon asked her where she'd been, she murmured vaguely about dining uptown with Zoë and a couple of boozy friends.

\* \* \*

Two weeks passed without a word from Owen. Claire was haunted by the 'Echo', that lambent pool at dusk, the two figures lost in their separate anguish, the daring of Moreno's vision. She waited tensely for Owen's call to Simon, for an announcement of the painting's sale, and indeed for mention of her own name. But Owen was silent, even on the social level: no invitation for drinks or dinner, no friendly salute from uptown, a curious silence for the usually gregarious Owen, according to Simon.

'Couldn't you call him?' Claire suggested.

'Not when he's working,' Simon answered ruefully. 'Owen's like that. You have to wait for the imperial summons.'

Claire had just arrived at the loft to begin her own morning's work. Now, sighing, she went into the bedroom, where she was organising the reviews of Simon's exhibitions, as well as feature articles about him which had appeared in magazines and newspapers over the years. A photograph in an old *Life* magazine, of a relaxed Simon and Olivia slouching in front of the window of this very loft, gave her a small jolt. She quickly read the accompanying article, which discussed Simon's achievement at some length, then praised Olivia for pursuing her own work, in her own studio across town, undaunted by her husband's fame.

She was contemplating this when she heard the phone ring. She was dimly aware that Simon's voice sounded strange on this call, first startled, then aggrieved, finally silent, as if he were being told something sobering. Irrationally, she feared that he was listening to bad news about herself: maybe some pal of his had glimpsed her and Zoë whooping it up with two amorous middle-management types in a French restaurant, and had decided to tell Simon the truth about his duplicitous girlfriend.

But after a few minutes Simon, looking tense and pale, came into the room to tell her that Owen was dead.

Claire stared at him. He settled heavily on the bed, and continued in a dull voice, 'That was the police who just called. They discovered my name among his things. It seems that somebody broke into his hotel room last night, believing that Owen was out. But he wasn't, he was in the room, and the burglar probably got scared...' He combed a distracted hand through his hair. 'So the guy attacked Owen; then fled. The cops haven't caught him yet. They took Owen to New York Hospital, God knows why, Lenox Hill is much closer. He died just two hours ago, from a bullet in the chest. The cops want me to go to the hospital.'

Claire came up beside him and put her arms around him. He looked to her like a child, baffled by some cruelty which had been levelled at him by the capricious adult world. Slowly she said, 'Simon, it must have been the painting that the burglar was trying to take. He must have known who his target was, or why would he have broken into Owen's hotel room? It must have been the painting.'

Simon lit a cigarette. His hands were trembling. 'How could he have known? Nobody knows except us and the Caron family and this guy who Owen wanted to sell it to. You didn't talk about the painting to anyone, did you?'

She swallowed. 'I sort of alluded to it, to Darby and Zoë. But I didn't give them very many details. And I asked them not to talk about it. They're my friends,' she finished feebly.

Simon was quiet a moment. 'Well, I don't think Darby would have babbled to anyone. He's pretty reliable. But what about your Zoë?'

She sighed. 'I just can't picture her talking about it when I expressly asked her not to. She's an unconventional woman, but in her own way she's as reliable as Darby.'

Simon stood up. 'It wasn't on the news. I asked the cop about it. He said they're keeping it quiet, for now, so that they can carry out their investigating, and because the hotel is terrified of scandal. Anyway, I have to go uptown, to speak to the police. Will you wait here for me?'

'Of course.' She touched his hand, which was icy, and still shaking. 'I wouldn't let you go through this alone.'

# Chapter Seventeen

Claire lay naked on the sweat-drenched sheets, longing for Simon's cool loft, yet unable to call him. Through some laziness, or a reluctance to indulge in the expense, she had never bought an air conditioner, but now she was regretting it, for this was a true New York summer night, dirtily hot and airless. From the street she heard sounds of bad temper: two men quarrelled for a while, then irritably gave it up; cars screeched; a baby cried miserably; a dog howled.

She pushed her clammy hair away from her face. Of course she would have had trouble sleeping anyway, but now, with the acrid air of shame breaking over her in waves, it was impossible. She got up and had a shower, but the moment she lay down again, the sweat returned, prickling in her hair and soaking the already sodden pillow. She could have been in

Bombay or Marrakesh; if she'd walked out now and seen palm trees drooping over whitewashed houses, a silent well, dogs sleeping in a dusty courtyard, it would not have surprised her. She tried to conjure up Constable's twilight landscapes with their umber skies and glimpses of cool streams, as though such sweet images might bring refreshment, but it was useless.

After Simon had returned from his police interview they had talked obsessively about Owen and the circumstances of his murder, until it seemed pointless to talk any longer. Then she had settled him into bed (depression and grief had exhausted him, and he slept the minute his head touched the pillow), after which she came here, to be by herself and think, because a terrible possibility had occurred to her.

She felt certain that Owen Kettlethorpe's violent death was connected to her own indiscretion; more specifically, to her gabbling to Zoë. Coke, and her own gauche naïveté, had loosened her tongue, until she had foolishly confided in a woman who lived an underground life, and who probably – no, certainly – had underworld acquaintances.

She breathed the humid air, helpless and afraid. Of course she could be wrong. Owen's murder could have nothing to do with herself and Zoë. But she feared the worst, feared that Zoë had talked about the painting to some pimp or gangster or drug dealer, who'd decided, simply, to lift it from Owen's hotel room, and when Owen himself had inconveniently appeared, well, there had been no choice...

This was crazy; she was dreaming some dark dream, indulging herself in a dark and groundless fantasy. There was no reason she should be jumping to these conclusions! But she had always been helpless against shame; shame was the one feeling she had always most dreaded, from her early days with her mother and father.

Other people complained of brutal or negligent parents, and that, for her, had always been the problem, because hers had *seemed* so loving. They were neither arid nor cold, they were not abusive, till night descended, of course, and the unspeakable was spoken, her mother's words smearing her like hot dirty hands. But that was to be forgotten in the morning, when her father would enter her bedroom, smiling anxiously, to protest their love for her. She would always recoil, for his protests were so *excessive*. And she had known, even as a child, the price he was exacting from her. Peace at all costs, her mother's peace of mind. She must not, must *never*, speak of what had transpired the night before. For her, the price of love was loneliness, a soreness she could not express and that they would not ease or even recognise. Nor could she recognise her parents as her enemies, for without them she would have no-one, not even herself, since her knowledge of herself was still too fragile, was still, in fact, in their hands.

The torrid air pressed down on her like a solid weight. It occurred to her that her mother, and she through her mother, was without history. Her mother's ancestry was like a path drowned in brambles. Muddy photographs of pale men with luxuriant beards, and women with piles of hair and high collars. There were only a few pictures of her grandfather whose eyes had been marvellously grey, and to whom a scandal clung, something to do with women and money; Cecily wouldn't speak of it. But who were they, all of them? Born in Russia, in *shtetl,* farm, or hovel, proud of their Marxist ideals, disdainful of religion, but without a country, a landscape to love, a home...

170

And her father's family? Her grandmother had been cruel to Gerald, contemptuous. Even as a child, Claire had registered the withering looks she had given him... Now she covered her eyes with her hands as though to expunge these pictures, but the thought of her father remained, her father as he was today, incontinent, gibbering. If Grandmother Fabienne were alive and could see him in his present condition would she give her customary shudder of delicate disgust, give her annoyed laugh, and turn away from this ruined man, her son?

She realised, suddenly, that her mother's drunken abuse of her was not the point. High drama, operatic displays, screams, the sound of glass shattering, all these were not the point. The point was her everyday life – shoelaces, a battered red bicycle, Central Park. She would travel with her parents in their car out to Long Island, passing suburban towns at twilight, lamp-light blooming behind windows – the tinselly, commercial meanness of those streets with their lawns and houses and shopping centres, the constricted lives, the neon signs on the Chinese restaurants – and Claire, even then, in the back of her parents' car, crying silently to herself, I will never live like this.

Even on carefree days, at the beach, or when her mother read stories to her, or her father took her to the museum, or when she was playing with her friends, even at those ostensibly happy times there was often a sadness, a dread, a kind of raging sorrow, in her throat, just behind her eyes, on the dark side of her heart. Everything that was supposed to reassure, to guarantee security – the world of dishwashers, televisions, supermarkets, bungalows – those things had always made her feel nearly faint with dread. Yes, she would leave this country, return to Ireland, maybe with Simon...

It was so pitilessly hot. She got out of bed and drank a

glass of iced water. All the vague feelings of unease which had dogged her throughout her life – the conviction that she had made some *faux pas* which would encourage people to reject her, her obsessive doubts about nothing at all – that nonsense was now put firmly in its place. What she was feeling now was no neurotic fear, it was the real thing. If she had indeed contributed to Owen's death through her frivolous behaviour, her desire to appear glamorous before her pals, her profligate tongue, then she had reason, real reason, to feel guilty now.

She took another handful of ice from the freezer and pressed it into the glass, poured water over it and drank again. She was wondering what had tormented her mother, compelled her to blunt herself with drunkenness and hurt her child. Cecily had worked at an interesting job, as a part-time English teacher for gifted high school students, and Gerald had loved her, or had seemed to. And there *had* been the good Cecily, affectionate and sweet. Perhaps Fabienne had driven her to drink? That imperious woman had not welcomed with joy the news that her son was marrying a Jew...When the drunken Cecily had reviled her small daughter, she'd called her a 'devious little bitch'. But now Claire realised that her mother was wrong. She, Claire, had not been devious, despite her fanciful stories and the guile she'd sometimes used to evade Cecily's anger. No, she'd been an innocent, and innocence was not a virtue. Innocence and naïveté, born as they are of so great a fear of darkness that one must gaze obdurately into ceaseless light, this was no virtue. Better to achieve some sort of wholeness, to understand darkness as well as light, to stop idealising people, instead of living afraid of one's own angry or greedy self, a fugitive in one's own precincts, rapt in some false dream.

She climbed wearily back into bed, throwing a glance at her desk, on which her Caravaggio book waited; she had been working well. But now she would try to forget about Owen, Zoë and her own folly, and simply, finally, sleep.

* * *

Just as she was easing into a shallow slumber, she was roused by a chorusing, ululating cry, as from many throats in unison. She went to the window and drew back the curtain. The sky was a deep gold, so bright that the windows across the street were kindled to fire. She looked away, into the park, and saw a great throng of men in brilliant white robes, kneeling on the grass under the trees. They were facing east, towards that blazing sun, towards the East River, and praying, she realised, to Mecca. Well, she said to herself, well. I think there is a lesson in this, in the radiant windows, the devout men, the sound of their voices. I don't know what the lesson is, not yet, but it will come to me later, I'm fairly sure.

# Chapter Eighteen

Simon had been interviewed by the police at the hospital where Owen had died, in an ugly, liver-coloured room. The detective who spoke to him was a handsome black woman with large green eyes and skin the colour of pecans. She was wearing a beige suit and pearl earrings; Simon thought she looked more like a stylish businesswoman than a cop. Her name was Jill Cooke.

She told Simon that they had found an empty easel in Owen's hotel room. Obviously a painting had been removed. She also told him that the police would have to release the news of Owen's death fairly soon, but for the moment they were conducting a private investigation, since, if a painting had indeed been taken, 'it might be making its way to the black market, and we don't want to alarm those who could be the principal dealers in such an operation.'

Simon confided to Detective Cooke that he himself had seen this painting, and he described it, but he didn't mention Claire; why should she be dragged in? Had they any idea who the murderer might be?

The policewoman sighed. 'There was only one witness. One of the hotel employees, a porter, saw a short man with reddish hair hurrying down the corridor on Mr Kettlethorpe's floor at about the time of the shooting. Does that description, a small man with reddish hair, sound familiar at all?'

'No,' Simon answered bleakly, reflecting that of course murder was a way of life in New York, but to his knowledge it had never soiled the art world in quite this way, a runnel of blood through it like those ribbons of scarlet in Sam Francis' paintings. But so much money was involved these days, he supposed it had to happen...

* * *

Days passed. Simon was painting now, working intently in the morning while Claire organised his papers. She was delighted that this should be so, that he should be fired with the need to paint, just as she was fired with the need to write, in the early evenings when she returned home. He was reluctant to let her see what he was painting, but did give her a charcoal portrait of her own face that he'd drawn from memory, a lovely small thing, the eyes solemn but the lips half-smiling.

One morning Simon suggested, out of the blue, that they should take his car for a spin in the country.

'You have a car? I didn't know you had a car!'

'I keep it in a garage by the river,' Simon explained, a little sheepishly. He was often worried about money but Claire considered that he must still have a lot, if he could afford to maintain a car in New York, which was nearly as expensive as maintaining a child.

It was a beautiful day, the clouds rinsed with a light that was not yet the hard, strident glare of New York in summer, but still vernal and sweet. And the trees were not yet the dusty khaki of high summer, but a tender spring green. He was talking about how colours, even their names, *viridian, celadon, emerald,* had excited him as a child, and while he spoke his hand kept dropping to her leg. She was wearing a long skirt without stockings, and he had pushed the fabric up to the top of her thighs so that his fingers could touch her skin, or else the white cotton of her underpants. After a while, with the trees glinting past and a smell of hay flowing into the car, she took off the underpants so that she was naked on the smooth seat, her skirt bunched up to her hips. He stroked her thighs, still discussing colour, *crimson, vermilion, coral.*

She had thought they were somewhere close to White Plains but they must have driven much further north, into real farm country. Simon turned onto a narrow road that sloped past calm fields, metal silos, farmhouses aproned with deep porches. Then there was a sort of meadow, and a stream into which willows dropped their ragged branches, and a smell of water, of loam and bruised grass. He stopped the car, and they got out and lay on the grass, she balancing over him, her hair falling into his face like the willows.

They made love for a long time, swaying and turning on the ground. Presently, lying on his back, staring intently at the stream, Simon began to cry, harsh tearing sobs. She laid her head on his chest.

176

He said in a hoarse voice, 'This stream reminds me of the "Echo", that pool in the foreground. And then I began to think about Owen...'

She considered her own heavy-heartedness, her secret anxieties and, of course, tears flooded her own eyes. But were they sentimental, self-pitying tears? She knew that if she were truly to do battle against her demons, and achieve an honest love with Simon, she must not keep secrets from him out of dread or shame. Also her reluctance to speak now, about Zoë's possible involvement in Owen's death, could impede the search for his killer. But she was still too afraid to utter the words, afraid of his anger, that he might reject her.

There was only one thing to do, something she'd hesitated over, again out of fear. But no more hesitation. Tonight she would speak to Zoë.

\* \* \*

Zoë was lounging on her settee, a tasselled carmine shawl thrown loosely around her shoulders. 'Come in, baby,' she summoned, extending a willowy arm, 'I am so happy you have decided to visit me.' She indicated the coffee table, on which there was a saucer bristling with half-smoked cigarettes, a number of abandoned glasses and cups, and a plate covered with crumbs, plum stones, and cheese rinds.

'I've been having a party with myself. I ate saucisson, cheese, and plums, and then I drank two whiskey coffees. But now I am bored, and longing for company.'

Claire lowered herself into the chair opposite. 'I thought you might be working.'

Zoë gave her throaty laugh. 'I took the night off. Yesterday

177

I was up till four in the morning with this out-of-town gentle-man who brought me to Area and then the Limelight. The Limelight was full of people wearing rings in their noses and navels, which made me wonder about getting new piercings done, in more intimate places. Could be good for business, *n'est-ce pas?* Shall I open a bottle of wine for us?'

'That would be nice.'

Zoë walked over to the drinks table, tottering slightly; she certainly was a little drunk, Claire decided, those whiskey coffees must have been pretty robust. The wine was a St Amour, which Claire remembered drinking with Simon and Owen the night she had seen the 'Echo'. Under the circumstances this coincidence was slightly disturbing, but she supposed St Amour was a suitable name for a wine favoured by Zoë. She swallowed some, impressed with its warm, light quality, and decided that it would be better to swing into her friend's spirit than to be glum and suspicious. 'Cheers,' she said, 'Thanks, Zoë.'

'Don't mention it, baby,' replied Zoë expansively, re-settling herself on the sofa. 'Didn't we have a nice time, the other night? Just like I said, nothing messy.'

'Speaking of the other night—'

'You're my best friend, honey.' Zoë's arm made another ample gesture in the air. 'And the other night taught me that not only can we talk together, we can actually *work* together.'

'What?' Claire was unnerved, remembering her own dangerous fantasies on that strange night. 'Zoë, I don't want to work with you! But I did want to talk about—'

Oblivious, Zoë slurped from her glass. 'I mean, I do enjoy all your art history stories, but there's no money in it, unless you inherit from some old collector who marries you at the last minute after you have lived with him in misery for a decade. I've got a much better idea. You are still young and good-looking.'

Claire stared apprehensively at her, realising that she'd already polished off her first drink and felt like another.

Zoë's fawn eyes were gleaming. 'Listen, baby, I cannot handle all the clients I have, and as you saw the other night, a lot of the work is just fantasy. Any practised girl can relieve a man in seconds; that's nothing special. What the boys really remember is the prologue, and then the slow dream afterwards. That's why my phone rings the whole time, all those voices anxious to know if I am still around. And with you and me operating together, business would boom. What do you say we order two beepers?'

'Beepers?' Claire asked faintly.

'Yeah,' answered Zoë impatiently, 'Like the cops and drug dealers use. Our initial investment could be two beepers. Half the calls for me I pass over to you – the sweet fantasy calls, nothing too hot-and-heavy, like that nice man the other night – and half your calls you pass over to me. We would become so famous we'd have to incorporate.' Her manicured finger followed invisible letters on the wall: 'Claire and Zoë's Fantasy Hothouse. I'd let your name come first just for alphabetical order.'

It was only at this moment that Claire realised Zoë was joking. She grinned. 'It's a great idea. And after all, we're living in this mercenary age, where the only thing that matters is money, and screwing the other guy. But we'd screw the other guy in a magnanimous and fruitful way.'

'*Precisement*, baby. We would be doing the world a lot of good. Many of those ruthless businessmen and politicians are just frustrated. They think it is money or power that will make them happy but really all they need is a little of the right kind of female company. An unsatisfied man is a sick man! Just imagine. You and I would be navigating the whole country through the sexual tempests of the late eighties. Have another drink.'

At that moment the intercom sounded. Zoë excused herself. Returning, she told Claire, 'It's my friend Lloyd, that man who gave me the fine cocaine that you and I and Darby Holland did the other night. He would like to come up here and have a drink with me.' She touched Claire's arm. 'Don't go away, baby. You might like to meet him.'

He was a short, wiry man with a bouncy walk, like a bantam-weight boxer. His thick ginger hair and agility suggested health, but his narrow face was dry, deeply scored, and marbled with the residue of adolescent acne. He had small eyes of a startlingly beautiful cornflower blue, and thin lips. Claire realised that he was one of those people whose looks immediately evoke an animal, in this instance a fox, or maybe a ferret. He was formally dressed, but his suit was black, like an undertaker's.

He insisted on taking them out for a drink at an old labourers' tavern on Grand Street called Roy's, which, with its beer-smelling darkness and *Budweiser* scrawled in neon above the bar, was fast becoming an anomaly, among the glinting bistros of SoHo these days. Looking around Roy's, Claire grieved a little for the lost SoHo of rough bars and warehouses mingling with galleries and studios, of sooty streets where you would be arrested by a spill of greenery in a window, and realise you had stumbled on one of those restaurants which had material-ised to feed the new pioneering artists, drowsy places where the raw beams were softened with dangling plants, and they came to settle their paint-spattered sleeves on the bar, and drink espresso or wine. That kind of restaurant decor, immense spaces, long bars, green vines tumbling over exposed pipes, was now an international cliché, but it had been new, then, and lovely, like walking into a vast bower. And even the cooking – spinach salads, avocado sandwiches, heavy puddings to blunt the sugar-lust of pot-smoking artists – had seemed charming and new.

Now that moguls and despots had displaced many of the artists, SoHo's original restaurants, Food, on Wooster Street and 162 Spring Street (avant-garde, then, to call a restaurant simply by its address), The SoHo Charcuterie – as well as working men's bars like Roy's, had disappeared or were disappearing, to be supplanted by expensive cafés which looked like they'd be more at home on Madison Avenue than down here in Bohemia. So Claire grieved a little, for her city, whose very spirit she feared might sicken, if the young and the workers and artists could no longer afford to live in it.

Lloyd bought them drinks: more red wine for Zoë and Claire, and a boiler-maker for himself. 'Here's mud in your eye,' he cried in a nasal New York voice. Then he laughed, showing yellow teeth.

At the next table an elderly man with wild eyebrows above a sardonic face was talking to a slender blonde girl. 'New York is no place for artists,' he cried angrily in a German accent, his eyes beneath their tangled brows full of grey scorn. 'I tell you, Esmé, you must go to a European country – Portugal is still fairly cheap, or Greece or Turkey – you must leave this vulgar land to breathe pure air in an ancient place, do you hear?' His hand fell on the girl's knee. 'I will arrange it for you.'

Lloyd flashed a smile at Claire. 'Hey, Zoë, maybe some night I'll take you and Claire out to dinner at Barney's. Claire, you know Barney's?'

Zoë snorted, 'Jesus, Lloyd, not *Barney's.*' She looked at Claire. 'Barney's is this old-fashioned steakhouse somewhere in New Jersey or something, where the waitresses dress like eighteenth-century housemaids, you know, with those corsets pushing up their tits and everything. And all the customers look like gangsters, or gangsters' floozies, and they all drink whiskey sours.'

The fair-haired girl at the next table, tranquilly stirring her drink, said, 'Ludwig, you are too much in love with the south. I *would* love to live in Europe, but the south is overpainted. Those Renoirs look so *syrupy,* like bonbons, and bullfighting is a macho travesty. I'm much more interested in the clean light of the north, Scotland or Norway, landscapes no one has painted, virgin territory.' She calmly removed his hand from her leg.

Lloyd drew a packet of Camels from the breast pocket of his black suit. 'It's nice to meet you, Claire. Any frienda Zoë's is a frienda mine, know what I mean? And I'm a real good friend to my friends, only Zoë don't always appreciate my friendship.' He gave Zoë's shoulder a playful push.

She said sharply, 'I'm a big girl, honey. If I happened to require your sort of help I would have looked for it a long time ago. As it is I am perfectly happy making my own arrangements for myself.' She scowled at the cigarette he was proffering, and took one of her own from her handbag.

Claire was astonished by this Lloyd, not so much by his vulgar looks or faintly sinister manner as by the sheer anachronism that he was. He was gangsterish in a nearly incredible way: the dagger-thin body in its black suit, the vulpine face with its harsh grin, that old-fashioned New York accent, all gave the impression that he had just stepped out of a James Cagney film. Now he got up to order another boiler-maker; Zoë and Claire had declined a second drink.

Claire said, 'Zoë, what does that man—'

'Never mind, honey. I'll tell you later.' But she hesitated, giving Lloyd, who was still up at the bar, her sidelong look. Then she murmured, 'Let's just say that he has got an operation, and he would like me to be involved in it. Only I do not like his business practices, and right now I am making good money and I am my own boss, so his protection or whatever does not interest me.'

'I see,' said Claire, only half-seeing. She was suddenly a bit afraid of Lloyd, and of this aspect of Zoë's life, which she could tell was deadly serious, and dangerous.

Suddenly Zoë's cool fingers touched her cheek. 'Claire, baby, you are looking pale. Is something the matter? Is it your father?'

Her father, denied the grace of a peaceful death. Gerald had taken her to the Metropolitan Museum, the two of them walking through Central Park in autumn, leaves rasping along the lozenged pavements, that tang in the air of mould and sap, a sombre pewter light in the sky, and her father asking, 'Are you warm enough, Claire-Bear, in your red coat?' Her father, and poor Owen...

She imagined Owen on the night he died, in his hotel room, sprawled in an armchair, drinking a brandy, and looking at the now lost Moreno. Maybe he had gazed at the painting with a mercenary relish, like a pirate gloating over his spoils. Or maybe he'd been moved by the forsaken couple, that sightless boy and voiceless girl, staring eternally out from their separate agonies? Or maybe he'd been thinking of other things, a pleasant meal he'd just eaten, his girlfriend in London, an article he meant to write. Then the door opening, and a figure, and then the two of them surprised, a kind of macabre comedy, Owen aghast, and the intruder, how had Simon described him, 'A short man, with reddish hair...'

Claire felt her bones grow cold. She looked away from Zoë, towards the bar, where it seemed that Lloyd had met some cronies. He was slouching against the counter, grinning with his sallow teeth at two men, both of whom were long-haired and skinny. Lloyd seemed small beside them. 'A short man, with reddish hair...'

'Zoë,' said Claire, 'Did you tell Lloyd about that painting, and about Owen Kettlethorpe?'

Zoë, lighting another cigarette, rolled her eyes. 'Well, I might have told him a little bit, because he has been bothering me so much lately, wanting me to work for him and all, so I might have said to him, "Lloyd, honey, you keep trying to impress me by telling me how much money you make, but I know that you are just small-time. There is a man I have heard about who can get a million dollars just by selling a little old painting." I only told him a little bit, honey, so he could see I was not impressed with him.' She tilted her head back, blowing smoke in the air. 'Why do you ask? Is something wrong?'

Claire swallowed painfully. Lloyd was still at the bar, drinking his high-octane drink and laughing with his friends.

She said in a low voice, 'Listen, Zoë, just don't talk to him about the painting anymore, do you hear? And don't tell him anything about this conversation; don't tell him I was asking about the painting, or about his connection to it, or anything.'

She clutched Zoë's hand, and continued sternly, 'You've let me down before. You are terribly indiscreet. But this time it's serious. Don't say a word, and, Jesus Christ, ease up on the drinks and the blow. They are probably clouding your judgement and making you do and say these stupid things.'

Zoë's eyes had widened. 'Okay, baby. I promise. But what is all this about?'

'I can't talk about it.'

Lloyd had come back. He was quite drunk now, looking at them with a kind of remote friendliness. 'Hey, girls, I think I'll go on home now. You sure you had enough to drink? All drinks on me, know what I mean? Hey, Zoë, if you was smart you'd reconsider my proposal. See ya later.'

He left, followed by the two men. Staring after them, Claire asked, 'Zoë, do you know Lloyd's second name?'

'No, I don't know hardly a thing about him, except that he lives in a penthouse somewhere in the West Village.' She gave Claire a chagrined smile. 'Sorry, baby.'

# Chapter Nineteen

Next morning Claire was just about to leave for Simon's loft when her phone rang. It was her mother. 'Claire? Your father has been taken to the hospital. He got – he was taken ill, much more ill, suddenly, and they – he was taken away in an ambulance. I called – I had to call the ambulance, he was delusional and – falling down. But it was terrible. He had fallen on the floor, I couldn't get him up, and he'd gone to sleep, but when he opened his eyes and saw the ambulance men looking down at him – I *had* to call them – but the look of terror on his face, when he saw them, and then he – began to cry...' As Cecily did, now.

'I'll meet you at the hospital,' Claire said, 'right away.'

She called Simon to tell him she would be late, then stopped at her letterbox on the way out, since for some reason the mail always arrived extraordinarily early in her building. Among the bills and ads was a letter from London, which she stared at, initially puzzled then slowly comprehending. She put it in her handbag, unopened.

* * *

After Claire had called, to tell him about her father's sudden decline, Simon went out to an Italian café that he liked, to drink an espresso and read the *Village Voice* and *ArtForum*.

Tilting back in his chair, listening to the hiss of the coffee machine, looking at a boy who was probably an art student with his crimson tights, canary jacket, and chartreuse hair, Simon thought about Claire, her father dying so cruelly. He would look after her when she came home to him.

There was so much he wanted to say to her. If he had only spoken sooner, about his own secrets... Now they had hardened into layers of deceit, and he was afraid.

He took from his wallet a letter he had placed there, over which he wanted to brood. It was from Ian Collins, the painter:

*Dear Simon,*

*You mind me saying you need a break? New York is fucking up your talent, my friend. Listen, my aunt in Ireland has just croaked (forgive the irreverence but false piety makes me puke, I mean I didn't even know the fucking woman) and she's left me her house, a nice big house I think, in the west of Ireland. I can't go there, I mean I don't want to, yet, I've got too much to do right now in the glorious Big fucking Apple, like prepare about forty exhibitions, etc. etc. etc. So*

187

*why don't you go? Go for a year? The light in Ireland is the*
*wildest and best in the world. Bring your friend Claire. If*
*she's a writer she can write anywhere, right? I'm serious,*
*Simon, I think NY is bad for your little soul right now. Call me.*
*Love and kisses,*
*Ian*

Simon folded the letter and returned it to his wallet. Claire had
often said to him that she intended at some point to leave
America, to live in Europe. As with himself, there were no
cords of loyalty, or patriotism, to keep her bound to the States.
Like himself, she was a kind of exile in New York, longing to
live in foreign places, feeling, in fact, that *America* was in some
ways alien to her. The paintings she loved were European, and
once she had told him that whenever she journeyed east,
across the Atlantic to Europe, it felt like a homecoming. And
for him it was the same. He *wanted* that light, *the wildest and
best*, light like mother-of-pearl, a dove-grey lustre chased with
gold. He wanted to leave New York and travel towards this
light, and paint it, paint his heart out.

There were images in his head, an iridescence like the glow
of forests or cathedrals, washes of almost transparent pigment
(perhaps even water-colour, since water-colour was 'as close
as a painter can get to pure light', according to Sean Scully,
an Irish painter living in New York!) So *alive*, this light, that a
figure is buoyed up on it, a tense, expectant figure, suspended
in a kind of *ether* of light... Yes, Ireland would be a redemption.
And he wanted Claire to come with him.

He would tell her everything, and then they would journey
far away from folly and error and madness. He touched his
pocket where the letter lay, as though it were a talisman.

\* \* \*

While he was walking home he saw Pat O'Dwyer again, standing on the corner of Spring Street and West Broadway – with a naked woman in his arms! But when Simon came closer he saw that she was one of those inflatable, 'anatomically correct' Latex dolls which lonely men are said to buy from the sex shops, for consolation.

'She's called Désirée,' Pat said cheerfully, 'Nice girl. Doesn't talk back.'

Her mouth was wide open in a perfect circle, obviously in order to accommodate a penis, but it gave her an unnerving look of terror, as though she were perpetually, silently screaming. She had fluffy fair hair and startled-looking blue eyes. Pat was clasping her round the waist in a tender way, as though about to give her a kiss; her arms flopped over his shoulders.

'What ever are you up to?' asked Simon.

'Making a delivery, for an exhibition by Luke Reilly. He's going to dress her up in cabbages. The exhibition will be called Culinary Erotica, or Food as Clothes as Sex as Art, or something like that. Anyway, old Désirée here will be the star of the show.'

'Jesus! I suppose it's a variation on Nikki de St Phalle's big lugubrious dolls?'

Pat laughed. 'Ah, Simon, I don't think Reilly knows enough about art to make connections as witty as that.'

The traffic light turned green, and they walked across the street, Désirée's head nestled comfortably on Pat's chest.

'I'm thinking of moving to Ireland,' Simon ventured.

'So am I,' Pat answered wryly.

Simon gave him a startled look. 'I thought New York was your spiritual home.'

Pat threw the doll over his shoulder. Simon nearly extended a restraining hand; the poor thing was so *naked*.

'Yes,' Pat answered, 'New York *is* my spiritual home, but I'm not breaking through. It's just too hard. I spend all day delivering sex dolls to posh galleries, and then at night I'm too knackered to do my own work.'

Simon said quietly, 'I once thought I could do something, strike a blow, for people like you, that I could do something to send up all the hype-dealers.' He gestured to the doll. 'But everything is so cynical these days...'

They were both silent a moment. Then Pat gave Désirée's waist an affectionate squeeze. 'Well, I had better get this girl indoors before she catches cold. 'Bye, Simon. Perhaps we'll meet in Ireland.'

\* \* \*

When Claire's father had arrived at the emergency room he was drawn away into the labyrinth of the hospital, as all incoming patients invariably are, trundled down corridors and into closed rooms, only he was more helpless than most. A nurse would tell Claire and Cecily when they could see him. After waiting an hour, they were finally directed to his floor.

They walked down the corridor, glancing apprehensively into every room. Presently they came to Gerald's, and the shock of seeing him marooned among indifferent strangers, the awful shock of seeing his familiar face on these clinical pillows, was more upsetting than Claire could have predicted.

And he was so terrified. His eyes were huge with terror.

When he saw them he let out a wail and cried, 'Oh, what did I do wrong? What did I do? Why are you punishing me? I promise I won't do it again! I promise–'

Claire, to her dismay, began to cry uncontrollably. Fortunately the room's second bed was empty, so that she could walk over to it, her back to her father, until she had composed herself again. When she returned, Cecily was clutching his hand and explaining, 'Gerald, darling, it's just that they can look after you better here. I haven't the equipment, or the strength, to take care of you, to lift you, and give you your bath and your medicines; do you understand?'

He murmured, 'Yes, yes, I understand,' but within a few seconds his face had once again grown slack with perplexity and fear.

A doctor, young, with a severe expression and glasses, appeared at the door and beckoned Cecily to follow him out into the corridor. Claire was left alone with her father.

It was a bright morning but the curtains were drawn, so that the room was full of a chalky darkness. She approached the bed where he was now sleeping, and placed her hand underneath his head. The eyes opened briefly, glaucous but still with deep brown irises, and stared at her.

As a child, Claire had loved to gaze at early photographs of him, amused and awed by this little boy, her *father,* wearing knickerbockers or short trousers, smiling shyly at the camera. He had told Claire that when he was small and had angered Fabienne she would chase him round and round the big dining table, until he exhausted her and they both collapsed into giggles.

His eyes closed again, and she realised that she was preparing to say goodbye to him.

# Chapter Twenty

Claire went with Cecily to the hospital cafeteria. It was lunch time, and Claire realised that she hadn't eaten all day, but the grey sandwiches and bedraggled salads could tempt neither of them. So they took only coffee, and settled with their steaming cups at a small table. Cecily said, 'The doctor told me that your father's deterioration is more rapid than most. He won't have much time...'

Claire touched Cecily's hand across the table. Then, to her own surprise, she suddenly asked, 'What is the true story, about the death of *your* father?'

Why had she asked such a question? For Claire, her grandfather had always been simply a photograph, of a handsome man in his youth, wearing a British army uniform – he had emigrated to England before travelling on to New York – and standing under a troubled sky which shone with the same grey lustre as his eyes. She had wanted to know more about him, but even as a child she'd understood that this subject was mysteriously taboo.

Cecily gave Claire a surprised look, and hesitated, but presently she began to speak in a dull, steady voice. 'I adored him, my father. He was very kind to me, and he seemed so glamorous with his English accent and beautiful suits. And we lived so well. It never occurred to me or to my childish mother that we were living *too* well, considering that this was the Depression, and my father had only a modest job in an insurance company, after all.'

She paused, fiddling with her coffee spoon. 'When I was only twelve he was taken to prison and I never saw him again. He died in the Tombs, of a heart attack, before his trial even began.'

The Tombs! That most desolate of prisons, and her grandfather had spent his last days there, in disgrace, exiled from his child. She pictured him waiting behind a grimy window, waiting with so little hope that he'd preferred to die. The Tombs reminded her of those Hogarth drawings of gibbering madmen, whores, and dissipated gentlemen all crowded into a dank prison room. What was that series called? The Rake's Progress...

'I suppose he was what they used to call a rake,' Cecily said just at that moment. 'He had embezzled money from the insurance company, and there was some scandal with a woman, or maybe many women... Anyway, it broke my mother's heart, and mine as well, and changed our lives. After his death everything was gone. I had lost not only him but all certainty, all security. We had to depend on the charity of relatives, who gloated a little, making remarks about my father that we had to swallow, since we were at their mercy. Strange how people are always wise after the event. And they'd been jealous of my father all along, so now they took their revenge, salt on our wounds.'

Claire was silent. Whatever intimations she might have had of the source of her mother's agony, these revelations were heart-stopping, as indeed they had stopped her grandfather's heart.

Cecily gave a hard laugh. 'Today some people might have considered him a hero. Rapacious businessmen are fashionable in the Reagan era, aren't they? Well, all I can say is that it wasn't easy. I tried to defend the memory of my father, and look after my mother, with all the fierceness of a young cub. But since I didn't know much about it I was easy prey to the taunts of my elders. You don't know how cruel to children the old can be!'

Claire stared at her, all her own childhood heavy in the air between them. She was glad her mother had explained her sorrow, but had the answer come too late for Claire to profit from it? Or were such revelations nearly always untimely? She felt as though she were caught in a hall of mirrors, or the cloud and shadow of a Piranesi dungeon.

But now, looking at Cecily, she realised how much she did love this sometimes brave, sometimes capricious woman who'd been both good and bad to her child, like all mothers, Claire presumed. But it was as though, at this moment, she were finally seeing Cecily as a *woman*, with all her own history, all her valour and sorrows and happiness, separate from Claire, not merely a mother, but *herself*.

Cecily said, 'I'm sorry, my dear, if I visited all my turmoil on you, instead of protecting you as a mother should. But please believe me when I say that all I want for you is happiness. You must keep working, you must remember that the only things which really matter are your work, and your autonomy.'

Claire considered this. 'And love? What about love?'

'Love is part of those things. When you are working, when you have joy of life, when you are *realising* your life, then naturally you can love another, because you have conceived a loving self. It happens as a matter of course. But you mustn't *lose* yourself in another person, you mustn't *drown* your true self in someone else.'

Claire said slowly, 'I got a letter this morning, from the Courtauld Institute, in London. They've said yes to my application.'

Six months before, Darby Holland had encouraged her to apply to the Courtauld for a grant, so that she could complete her Caravaggio book in London. She had submitted samples of her writing, and a description of her project. And they had said yes, they would cover all her expenses, she could have a year with them, to conduct her research and write her book. They would buy her a plane ticket, but she must fly out within six months.

She had actually forgotten all about the application, because she'd thought she wouldn't have a chance. Six months ago she hadn't even begun the book, so that all she could submit to the Institute were her *ArtDimension* pieces. But this morning she had learnt that the Courtauld were actually impressed, they had decided she would write a good book, they *wanted* her to complete it under their auspices!

To Claire's dismay, her mother's face was settling back

into its familiar, indignant pout. For all her talk of work and independence, she was reproachful now, guilt-inflicting, clutching at her daughter's soul.

'How *could* you think of leaving me?' Cecily cried, 'going off to another country and leaving me all alone! You are so *heartless*, Claire. Your father–'

Claire was pleased to register that she was not trembling with fright and rage, as she used to whenever Cecily had tried to engulf her in the past. She answered calmly, 'Mother, you told me today that Dad has about three months. I will wait with you here in New York until he dies. And after that you will be fine. You are not yet old, you're healthy, and you'll have Dad's pension from the university and all your savings to support you. And you have a daughter who loves you and who will travel to London, to work, and to realise her life's dream, as you have advised her to do.'

Cecily bowed her head, but she also extended her hand and grasped Claire's hand across the table. 'Yes,' she said.

* * *

Claire returned home, called Simon, and told him that she was exhausted and would like to have a snooze.

He said, 'Fine, darling. Don't worry about work today. Come over this evening and we'll go out to dinner. There's a new restaurant in TriBeCa that I'd like to try.'

She slept, and dreamt that she and Simon had gone to a department store, to buy a suit for him, but he kept throwing the clothes on the floor (they were impossibly ornate, jackets with electric pink lapels, popinjay trousers stitched through with gold thread, sequins-adorned waistcoats). 'They're not *me*,' he kept saying exasperatedly, 'They're just not *me*.'

'This one is you!' cried Claire, retrieving a brocade coat from the floor. They examined the label, which read *A Simon Brady Original*. Then there was an insistent, incessant ringing; her eyes opened and she stared out the window. It took her a moment to realise that she was hearing her phone. She answered it, groggily.

'Claire,' said Darby's voice, low and urgent, 'Zoë's been beaten up.'

'What?' She was struggling up through the murk that an afternoon sleep often produced in her. 'What, Darby?'

'I'm here at Zoë's place. She won't let me call a doctor. She wants to see you. I was just passing by and I decided to visit her, and when I came up... She's been beaten up and the apartment is a wreck. She won't talk to me. She's saying she wants to see you.'

'Dear God. Darby, please stay with her. How bad is she?'

'She'll be okay. She's more worried about the cat than herself. We can't find the fucking cat. Anyway, come over, as fast as you can.'

# Chapter Twenty-One

The door was opened not by Darby but by Zoë's friend Patricia, whom Claire had met once before, at a birthday party for Zoë in a gay bar, since Patricia was lesbian. She was also a woman of almost unreal beauty, black, with enormous eyes, a long throat, and a figure at once delicate and rounded, like certain nymphs in Grecian statuary whose draperies are moulded to their sloping shoulders, high breasts, and tiny waists. Like Zoë, she was a kind of freelance call-girl.

'Come in, Claire. Zoë and I were supposed to go shopping today; that's why I'm here,' she explained in a subdued voice, 'Darby's in the bedroom with her.'

The living room looked nearly normal, since it was never tidy, but there was something, a charge in the air, an impression of menace. Then Claire registered certain details: one of Zoë's china doll lamps lay face-up on the floor, the shattered bulb beneath its flounced dress looking horribly like a miscarriage. A green feather boa, one long black evening glove, and a black dress had been thrown in a corner, and a bowl was overturned on the coffee table, spilling grapes and overripe peaches onto the carpet.

Patricia said, 'Go in, Claire, she's been waiting for you.' It was as though Patricia were the receptionist in this drama, decorously welcoming guests and directing them to the central chamber.

Zoë, wrapped in a white silk dressing gown, was lying on the bed, her head buttressed by a mound of pillows. The mattress was bare; all the bedclothes had been dragged off onto the floor, presumably by her attacker. Darby, balanced tensely beside her, was stroking her hand. The curtains were drawn, plunging the room into a kind of gloaming, and reminding Claire of her father's hospital room, another dimly lit place of pain, where she had been only that morning.

As she approached the bed she saw that Zoë had two black eyes, a livid bruise on her right cheek, and a broken lower lip. Her legs, exposed at the knee below the white silk, were also bruised, with one particularly nasty-looking black-and-violet splotch on the right calf. There was a basin of pinkish water and a blood-covered towel on the floor at Darby's feet.

'Hi, baby,' said Zoë in a furred voice, 'Nice weather we been having.' She tried to smile but winced instead. Then she said to Darby, 'Honey, I want to talk to Claire in private. You go out and have a cup of tea with Patricia for just a little while.'

Darby left, giving Claire a grim and puzzled look. She took his place on the bed beside Zoë. 'Who did this to you?' she asked, taking her hand as he had done.

'Baby, I cannot tell you how much I want a cigarette and a glass of vodka, but my lip is all cracked. Darby was such a lamb, sponging my face. Where is my cat? What did he do to my cat?'

'What did *who* do?'

'Lloyd.' Zoë shuddered. 'You want me to tell you exactly what that rat did to me?'

'Yes.' Although she wasn't certain, not at all certain, that she really did want to know.

'He raped me, with a bottle. Don't look at me like that, baby, it wasn't a *broken* bottle, but it did hurt. I just could not defend myself. He is a small man but *strong*, and those arms of his move fast as snakes. You know how it is.'

'Yes,' answered Claire, as if she did. 'Was it because you were refusing to work for him?' Why was she asking these questions, when she already knew the answers?

Zoë squeezed her hand. 'He came here today and told me about the painting. You know, honey, Lloyd shot that man. He found out where his hotel was...' She was quiet a moment then gave a snort of bleak laughter. 'Did you know that walking into a hotel and going up to someone's room is the easiest thing in the world, despite all those security men and cameras and everything? It was easy for Lloyd and in my business it is easy, too. Security guards are just like flies you can brush away if you are well-dressed and confident enough.' Sighing, she touched her sore lip, and her lashes fluttered as though she might sleep. But then, without Claire having to prompt her, she resumed.

'So Lloyd went to the hotel. He thought Kettlesomething was out, I don't know why, but when he broke in...'

'I know. Kettlethorpe was there, and Lloyd shot him.'

'And then he threw a sheet over the painting, and walked out with it, just like that! Like I was saying before, *nobody stopped him*. It is so strange, a man walking through a crowded foyer with a painting under his arm, and not even one person saying, "Excuse me, Mister, but who the hell are you and what is that big square thing your are carrying out of our hotel?" but that's how it was.'

'What did Lloyd do with the painting?'

'He panicked after he got home. You know, he had not meant to kill anybody. So when he was back in his apartment and he could think a little, he realised that he had really fucked up and now the painting was just too hot to handle. So he burned it.'

'He *burned* it?'

'He told me that he lives in one of those buildings with a big incinerator in the basement, and a chute on every floor. So it was easy for him to just razor-blade the picture out of its wooden backing or whatever, roll it up, and throw it down the chute, as if it was only garbage. Then he chopped up the wood and threw *that* down, too.'

Claire was astonished by the rage she felt. So Owen had died for this, for char and cinders. Lloyd had destroyed a human life and, with it, an example of the art which had sustained that life. The 'Echo' would have lived forever, and it would have been a homage to Owen, but now it was lost, lost. She pictured the furled canvas tumbling down an incinerator's metal throat, borne along on an eddy of hot air, to disappear in a rush within the furnace alongside a mess of domestic rubbish, the detritus of meals, Coke and beer bottles. Owen had given her a small photograph of the 'Echo', which he had taken himself with an ordinary camera, and now that amateur-ish picture would probably be the last and only remnant of Moreno's great painting, the only tribute to his vision of bereavement and beauty.

Zoë squeezed her hand again. 'Jesus, I need a cigarette. Anyway, Lloyd told me the whole story, almost like he was proud of it. And then he said I would *have* to work for him now, since if I didn't he would tell the police that I had killed Kettlethorpe. You see, honey, Lloyd believes that Kettlethorpe must have been a client of mine. That's how he thought I knew about the painting. How else could I have known? I never told him about you and Simon.' She gave another dark laugh. 'Yeah, I guess you can say I have been at least a little bit discreet – you and your boyfriend are in no danger from that bastard.'

Claire could not speak. Zoë touched her swollen lip again. Suddenly she cried, 'Lord, I was such a fool that day when I spilled the beans to Lloyd. There I was boasting to him, "You think you are so fine but I know somebody who makes more money in an hour than you could in a whole year. His name is Kettletop or something and he is a famous art expert and he is in New York right now, in a hotel with this million-dollar painting..."'

The room was darkening. Claire could not see Zoë's bruises anymore, only the indistinct oval of her face, and her dark hair spread out on the white pillows.

'Lloyd said he would give me just a little taste of what would happen to me if I talked to the cops. And this is what he did.' She squeezed Claire's hand painfully hard. 'Listen. I am not going to a hospital, and I am not talking to the police.'

'But you *should* see a doctor. You might have internal injuries–'

'Patricia will take care of me. I am going tonight to Patricia's room at the Chelsea. And then as soon as I am well again I go home to Louisiana.'

Claire peered through the ashen gloom, trying to read her friend's face. 'Zoë, you don't have to flee. The police will put Lloyd away. Simon spoke to a woman cop, a nice woman. She'll look after you. Don't you see? We have to make sure that Lloyd is put away. Besides, if you went away we would miss you terribly, Darby and I and your other friends...'

'I love you, too, baby.' Zoë managed a chuckle. 'But you don't need me so much anymore. You used to be so romantic and up in the clouds, but now you are finally settling into your own skin. You have been writing your book, which is everything.'

Startled by this echo of her mother's words, Claire asked again, 'What about love?'

'Love, too. But you need to have your own life, 'cause when you are all helpless and dependent it only brings anguish. Anyway, give me some time. Maybe I will talk to that lady policeman.' Claire felt rather than saw her turn her head to the window. 'But right now all I want is to go to sleep...'

\* \* \*

When she entered the bright living room, where Patricia and Darby were conferring on the couch, the light scalded her eyes, and she felt suddenly faint. Darby grasped her arm. 'I'll take you home.'

Only when he had brought her back to her own apartment did she realise she had eaten nothing all day, literally nothing. She'd taken no breakfast, and only coffee with her mother at the hospital.

'You've got no food in this fucking place,' Darby muttered disapprovingly, frowning into her cupboards. 'Wait a while, silly Pumpkinhead.'

He threw on his coat and went out, returning a quarter of an hour later with two brown parcels. He bustled about in the kitchenette for another few moments and emerged finally with a bowl of fragrant soup, a plate of pâté and mustard and gherkins, French bread, and a square of some hard cheese.

Claire drank the soup avidly, her hands trembling; then, calmer but still ravenous, she attacked the pâté and eventually the cheese. At one point the phone rang but she let Darby answer it. It was Simon, and Darby spoke to him at some length, but she was too hungry and tired to care what they was saying.

When he came back to the table he said, 'Hey, leave something for me, will you?' She passed him the plates, smiling apologetically. He'd bought a bottle of red wine along with the food, which he opened now, pouring them each a glass. 'I told Simon you might be along later,' he said through a mouthful of cheese and bread, 'And he wanted you to know that he'd be glad to come here if you'd prefer. I didn't tell him about Zoë.'

'Thanks, Darby.' And she proceeded to describe her fraught day, and her conversation with Zoë, there being no need, anymore, to keep these things a secret.

Darby, art historian and *aficionado*, focused on the painting. 'So it's gone, burnt, destroyed! Christ, what a pity. And you're pretty sure it was genuine?'

'Fairly sure. All that remains now is a photo. Here...' She got the picture from her desk and placed it beside his plate. 'Don't smudge it, Darby. You know how messy you are.'

'Shut up, Pumpkinhead,' he answered casually, lowering his wineglass to examine the photograph.

Suddenly she was feeling terribly drowsy. It must be the food and wine, she thought, devoured with such urgency after a day of fasting, and of course the emotional tumult she had endured since morning... The plumbing groaned, a dull tremor shook the windows as a truck passed below, the fridge throbbed then shuddered into silence. Where, she wondered blearily, was Zoë's cat...?

\* \* \*

She must have slept, but only very briefly, because when her eyes opened she was still at the table, and Darby was still staring at the photo of the Moreno. At that moment he glanced up, his long crooked face unsmiling. 'Look at it again,' he said.

'What?'

He pushed the picture across the table. 'Just look at it again. The last time you saw this painting you were thrilled to have met Kettlethorpe, and you'd had this romantic meal with lots of wine, and you were in his gorgeous hotel room with Simon, and they were probably wooing you with flattery, the whole shebang. Now just look at it again; *study* it.'

Suddenly dry-mouthed, she did as he asked. There it was, the dense wood, the dark pool, the suffering boy, Echo's eyes wide with desire and desolation... Claire swallowed. She looked up, had a gulp of wine, then resumed her study. She could hear Darby breathing, smell his odour of soap and wool. All such things, smells, noises, colours, were suddenly heightened; the air itself seemed to vibrate. She heard Darby cough, heard a shout from the street. She looked up again.

Darby said, 'You know how sometimes you switch on the TV to a costume drama, a Robin Hood film or a Western, but you know immediately that the movie was made in, say, the nineteen-fifties, despite the antique costumes? The women, for instance, subscribe to the feminine ideal of their own time, not the period of the film. So you switch on the television to this Robin Hood film and you know that you are supposed to be looking at Maid Marion, but her red lips and stylised eyebrows and those cylinder-like boobs that were so popular in the Fifties tell you instantly that the movie was made in nineteen-fifty-six or something, and if the actress resembles anybody, it's Marilyn Monroe, not Maid Marion...'

Claire said quietly, 'But the girl in this painting has the typical Moreno face, doesn't she? White skin and huge black eyes.'

'It's not the face so much. Think of another Moreno. Think of his "Saint Catherine".'

She pictured Catherine's round shoulders, her dimpled arms. Then she smiled dryly, bitterly. 'This girl is just too skinny, isn't she? This Echo is just too skinny, almost like a fashion model.'

He poured them more wine. 'They liked 'em fleshier in those days. You never see a defined musculature in Baroque nudes. Those bodies are just too opulent to show sinews and bone structure. Think of Rubens, for Christ's sake, or even your Caravaggio.' He touched the photograph. 'This is simply a modern body. It's unmistakable. I mean, whoever painted this is pretty good. The brushstrokes, the theatrical lighting, Narcissus' eyes directly confronting the viewer, that sense of humanity, of pathos... All very Baroque, very authentic. Except for this one little thing.'

206

# Chapter Twenty-One

'But Owen thought it was real...'

Darby looked steadily at her. 'Well, the big-shot experts are often lax. They become complacent, think they know more than they actually do. While it's us hungry types who really work to see properly.' He paused. 'Or maybe Kettlethorpe's critical eye was becoming occluded. Maybe he was growing tired – or maybe *he* was a fraud.'

Claire said quietly, 'Berenson used to authenticate fakes on purpose, as a send-up.'

'Not just a send-up, Pumpkinhead. You're so naïve. Berenson had vast expenses. I Tatti wasn't exactly a tenement.'

She stared at him. 'If what you suspect is true, it means that Kettlethorpe made a fool of me on purpose. I was so flattered, so moved and pleased. And he exploited that. Oh, how could he?'

Darby tugged at his eternally rumpled hair. He repeated, 'You're so naïve. If you're not careful, Pumpkinhead, you'll grow into a cynic. That's what happens to you Candide types. You insist that everyone's perfect and then when you learn that they're just human you become all sour and disaffected. What did you expect from Owen Kettlethorpe? Everyone knows he was a wily old con artist.'

'Well, I thought he– He seemed so sure about this picture, and it *is* so beautiful. Who do you think might have painted it?'

'Who knows? Maybe Kettlethorpe himself.'

She said glumly, 'Perhaps he drew me into all this because he wanted me to write about it for the magazine.'

'Maybe. For credibility.' He seemed to hesitate. 'I wonder how many people were in on this, if it was a con job? That French family, the Carons, of course, if they exist. And maybe even Brady.'

'*Simon?*' Her stomach turned over. 'Of course not. He's a painter himself. He'd never desecrate what is so dear to him, never! And he wouldn't do it for money. He has plenty of money...'

Darby said nothing.

'And it would mean that he was lying to me from the beginning. It would mean that our whole relationship was counterfeit. And I *feel* it isn't so, it couldn't be...'

Darby poured out the last of the wine. 'Let's not jump to conclusions. We're not even sure that the painting isn't authentic. It's just a feeling.'

'A feeling,' she repeated faintly, touching the photograph on the table.

# Chapter Twenty-Two

After Darby left, Claire did not go to Simon's loft. He phoned again, at midnight, and she told him she was close to collapsing after her hard day, and would see him tomorrow. She hadn't the energy, or the heart, to discuss her new unease about the 'Echo'.

But then she couldn't sleep. She tried to think of pleasant things. She had told Darby about the Courtauld, and after congratulating her he'd asked to see some of her recent work. She gave him the introduction to her Caravaggio book, which he read with his swift, practised eye, and praised. Anyway he muttered, 'Not bad at all,' which, from the dour Darby, was a glowing compliment.

But nothing could stop her thinking of Owen, of the repulsive Lloyd, of how indiscreet she'd been with poor Zoë, of her disgraced grandfather, her dying father, what would happen between herself and Simon when she went to London, the painting buckling in the flames...

* * *

Next morning, Claire got dressed in her lightest clothes (the radio, with an almost sadistic relish, had predicted 'a scorcher'), and hastened off to Simon's.

Emory, her junkie friend, sidled up beside her as she was walking past King Tut's Wa-Wa Hut. His eyes looked huge and glassy. 'Hi,' he said in a strange, light voice, 'Hi, sweetheart. Want to come with me?' He pointed at the sky, already hard and cloudless with incipient heat. 'Up there is where it's at. I believe in crack 'cause I can't afford smack.' He gave a shrill laugh. 'Won't take long. Sing my song?' He tottered back and she was afraid he might fall.

'Hey, Emory,' she said, 'Go on and crash somewhere. I can't talk with you when you're like this. Go away.' She was surprised, but not displeased, by a new firmness in her voice.

She hurried west, towards First Avenue, but on the corner she nearly stumbled over a man who was on his knees in a stiff and uncomfortable position, his forehead pressed against the asphalt. It was as though he were abject, or offering homage to an idol. She stopped and stared.

Suddenly a voice said, 'I think you must not worry.'

Looking up she saw an elderly man with a thin Slavic face, slouched in the entranceway of a brownstone. His arms were folded over his chest; he wore round glasses and a sardonic smile. 'I think you must not worry,' he repeated in his pleasant, accented voice. 'This gentleman is all right. Maybe he is a Muslim, praying.'

Claire said, 'If he were Muslim he'd be facing east.'

This man's lean face smiled again. 'Ah, well, then let us elaborate. Maybe he is indeed a pious Muslim who for some reason became inebriated, so that he has forgotten which direction is east.'

She looked down again at the man in the gutter, at his rigor of abjection. 'I was afraid he might be sick. He's so still and *wooden*.'

The bespectacled man gave a lugubrious chuckle. 'I shouldn't be concerned. I live in this house, and I have observed this gentleman many times. Let us conclude that he is merely taking his siesta.'

'I see.' Claire appraised the old man. 'So,' she said, 'you are a cynic, then?'

He laughed, less ruefully than before, more with genuine amusement. 'No, my dear. Merely a realist.'

'I see,' she said again. 'Well, good bye.' And, walking around the bowed man, she made her way onwards.

* * *

In the late seventeenth century Antonio Varacci painted 'The Suppliant', in which the subject is alone and bitterly debased. His tattered robe reveals a birdlike chest and wasted left thigh, his unkempt beard falls almost to his knees, and he extends his filthy arm in the mendicant's gesture. But the artist makes it clear that this man is by no means poor in spirit: an uncanny, sourceless radiance illumines his face, firing the gaunt cheeks, glowing from the large eyes, and about the whole figure there is an impression of dignity, and pathos. Claire thought of The Suppliant as she walked up to Simon's loft, associating him with Emory and the man she'd seen crouched in the street, but also with her father, and Zoë, and somehow with herself. Her hands were trembling, and she was close to tears.

\* \* \*

Simon immediately took her in his arms, and she mumbled against his chest, 'It was a terrible day, yesterday. I'll tell you all about it, later, but for now I'd prefer just to work, and then have a sleep. We can go out to dinner tonight, if you'd like, and then we can talk. But for now I can't.'

'Of course.' He caressed her hair. 'Anyway, my accountant is coming here this morning. Work as long as you can, then close the door and go to bed.'

\* \* \*

After sleeping all afternoon, she finally got up with a faintly throbbing head. Simon was out. She found a message from him on the dining table, explaining that he'd gone to buy brushes at Pearl Paint, and would be back at about seven o'clock.

She had a shower, then saw that the pins she'd worn in her hair the night of her outing with Zoë were still in a little cup by the basin, and she used them to put her hair up again. She was feeling a desire to do these pointless, frivolous things, to mess with her hair, to make up her face a bit with rouge and powder, to dress slowly and carefully, like a dreamy adolescent. All so that she wouldn't have to think. She felt nearly punch-drunk from thinking about all the weird things that had been happening lately: her overloaded brain could not begin to make sense out of it all.

When Simon came back they had a glass of wine in the kitchen, and she told him first about her father and her long talk with Cecily. Then, slowly, she described Zoë's plight and her own place in it. He looked grim and shaken, but to Claire's relief he did not reproach her. She could not talk to him about Darby and the painting. She tried, but the words grew thick in her throat and would not come. 'Let's go to the restaurant and talk more there,' he proposed, and she said yes.

The sky was growing dark as they walked through TriBeCa, under the metal canopies of warehouses, closed and silent at this time of evening, except where a glimmer of light under an iron door revealed the presence of a gallery or loft. A thin fog mantled the streetlamps, and the wind was seasoned with brine from the river. Along Hudson Street they saw a broad window in which a burnished light flared briefly, then died. They stopped at some distance to stare and it happened again, a curious golden light blooming, glowing, then guttering and dying. They walked closer, looked through the glass, and saw two men working with lathes and blowtorches at a trestle table. A spume of fire sprayed out from beneath their gloved hands, illuminating their arms and helmeted faces, but keeping the vast room behind them, full of blackened and ancient-looking equipment, in shadow. Simon murmured, 'It's like your favourite period, isn't it? Like a Baroque painting of a forge, *chiaroscuro*.'

She gazed in at the two men, at the eerie picture of them labouring like this so late in the evening when every other place was shuttered and still, and at the room so full of darkness and sputtering light, like a smithy, or a forge, as Simon had said. And at that moment, as she was gazing, something broke in her, something like a seal that had kept a certain truth, closed in, knowledge that she'd always had, really, so that the releasing of it now, the pouring of it out from that sealed place into her consciousness, had about it a quality not of revelation but of inevitability and weary recognition: *Ah, yes,* she said to herself, *ah, yes, this is the truth, after all.*

She touched the window and was startled to feel how chill it was, even on this very warm night, and then she said, quite calmly, looking not at Simon but still through the glass at the two men, 'You painted the "Echo and Narcissus", didn't you?'

She heard him inhale sharply, then a rasping sound as he lit a cigarette. 'Yes,' he said simply.

She closed her eyes and settled her forehead against the window. The light quickened and died. She straightened, looked at him, and said in a low voice, 'Maybe the thing I loathe most is how you asked me to recite the whole myth to you, in that restaurant with Owen. And, oh God, how I threw myself into the telling! Like a schoolgirl pleased that the big important people were noticing her at last.'

'Claire–'

She made a silencing gesture, then looked again through the window where shards of fire were once more spraying from under the men's blowtorches. Her mind was moving too swiftly, like a car careering, all that speed in your hands, and the terrible clarity. 'I see now,' she continued quietly, 'I see when it began. You probably did genuinely want someone to organise your papers, but when Darby suggested me for the job, and you realised that I had actually written on Moreno for

214

*ArtDimension*, you saw how you could work me into your design, yours and Grandfather Kettlethorpe's.' She was feeling something she could only think of as blackness, as though she had been plunged into an oubliette, into some desolate place where there was nothing for her, no possibility of rescue, only loss. 'I believed you, all your talk about grace, and love. I made love with you. And Owen's deference to me, how he praised my judgement, undimmed by academic jargon...'

'Claire,' he tried again, but again she silenced him with a gesture. 'I'd have been ruined, humiliated, if Owen had revealed my part in this, and I'd written about it, and then someone discovered the truth. Silly, self-important girl, so proud to be accepted by the big boys, an eyewitness Baroque specialist singing the praises of your con job.' She paused. 'And I really loved that painting. I believed it was real.' Tears blurred her vision for a moment. 'And you took that from me, too,' she whispered, 'The painting, too.'

He said with a tremor in his voice, 'Your conclusions might be wrong. You should let *me* tell the story.'

But she ignored him. 'You chose me on the basis of my "Saint Catherine" article, didn't you? The *ArtDimension* readers were used to seeing my name connected with Moreno. You arranged it so meticulously. You would convince me that your phoney picture was authentic. Then I'd write an article praising it for *ArtDimension*, which would serve as an official benediction, although I'm not a famous scholar...' She swallowed. 'But I suppose that was the reason you chose me. Stupid me, nearly thirty but still so naïve and easily dazzled, so dependent and gullible. I was perfect! No big deal myself, but with access to a prestigious magazine. Seducing me was effortless. And after you'd seduced me I'd see only what you wanted me to see.'

He said brusquely, 'Seducing you, as you inaccurately describe it, was never a factor in our scheme. My love for you came unexpectedly, and it has always been separate, totally separate, from anything involving the painting.' He threw down his cigarette and crushed it under his shoe. Fire glowed again in the silent forge behind them. She cried, 'But *why*, Simon? *Why* did you do it?'

He looked hard at her, then pointed to a small bar on the corner. 'Claire, please, come with me into that bar. Come in with me and have a drink, and let me explain. Do that much for me, for the two of us, before you decide anything.'

She hesitated, then reluctantly, sullenly, said yes. Sad and separate, they walked across the street.

\* \* \*

'Last winter, when Owen came to New York, we dreamt up this fantasy, about how we would love to expose just how mercenary, and meretricious, and indeed *counterfeit* the whole art scene had become.' He paused, remembering that curious day, so long ago, how he had drawn his curtains against the dusk while Owen, half-mad from coke and the transatlantic flight, had chattered behind him. It had been his pre-Claire period, when things were bleaker... 'Anyway, we began to devote all our time together to discussing this wild dream, and over a time it came to seem more and more possible.'

Claire waited, hands clasped on the clammy table. The bar was dank-smelling, a fake Irish bar with green-coated leprechauns frolicking on the walls, but with mainly black customers. Simon went on, 'What we wanted was to reveal how venal, how money-mad, the whole scene is, and also how pretentious and often incompetent the critics and so-called experts can be.'

She said bitterly, 'I'd have been included in your group of incompetent so-called experts, if I'd written that piece for *ArtDimension*. You'd have exposed me as a charlatan, or a star-struck ninny, or something equally flattering.' She looked around wildly. 'Oh, God, what am I doing here? I should go, now, before–'

He caught her wrist. 'Just hear me out. That's all I ask. Claire. Please.'

She looked at him. He continued, 'With the "Saint Catherine" controversy, Owen was able to show me how easily it could be done. Owen really did believe the Catherine was genuine, despite the protests of that French critic, who I gather is really arrogant, a typical example of the bombastic intellectual phoniness that prevails among those people. Paintings are just a means to flaunt their superior knowledge; they don't *feel* them at all. But everyone bowed to Owen over the "Saint Catherine", because of his name. He said I should have seen how all the critics fawned.'

'I know, Simon. I wrote an article about that painting, remember? So you realised that if you manufactured another controversy, this time surrounding a picture you knew was a fake, you could – Owen could – triumph over the little snobs just as he'd done with the Catherine.'

'Yes, only this time there was an agenda. We were never intending to get away with it forever. We were going to reveal the truth. Don't you see? Deceit and concealment were not the point. The truth was the point.' He lit another cigarette. Claire was tempted to stalk out, to leave him alone in this glum bar, but despite herself she was still crying out for an answer, for deliverance, for a *reason*. So she waited.

'Darling, I didn't know *you* when we concocted this scheme. We were full of righteous anger and exhilaration, and we were heady with it. We thought we'd create this incredible scandal and make them all feel like fools, as though people's work and reputations wouldn't be implicated in what we intended to do.'

'You thought you were crusaders,' she said contemptuously, 'You didn't care who you trampled on. And you had the gall to hate *their* grossness...'

'Yes, we thought we were heroes.' He opened and closed his hands on the table. 'But I never meant to hurt you. And as I've said, our intimate relationship was never an aspect of this. Never was there a design that I'd seduce you to make you more malleable or whatever.' He smiled wryly. 'I think I really did begin to love you that very first day when you came to work, when we had lunch, the nice wine I'd bought specially, because I'd liked you so much at the interview, not letting myself think too much beyond that, really, just wanting to see you again. But at the lunch table, when you began opening up and telling me all about yourself in that bizarre nineteenth-century way of yours, all I wanted—'

He looked down, and she thought he might be fighting tears. Of course it occurred to her that despite what he had just said she had not, actually, told him all about herself, either at that first lunch or after. It had taken her far, far too long to confide in him about her night with Zoë and the two men, and about her indiscretion concerning Owen. All her life she had practised this particular kind of guile, altering her history, concealing, because she was afraid of what might happen if she were seen for herself. She looked around at this fake room, at the walls decorated with paper shamrocks and capering leprechauns, at the few customers, all men, talking listlessly at the bar. All she had ever wanted was to be loved for herself, but by her reluctance to reveal the dark side of herself she had rendered her own dream unattainable. Until Simon. With him alone a real intimacy had nearly become possible for her. Although now, ironically, it was *his* dark side, too long suppressed, and his deceit, which were blighting the air between them.

He went on, 'I will tell you how we meant to involve you. Both Owen and I really did admire your writing, and your intelligence–'

'Why, thank you,' she said sarcastically.

'–and so we decided that if *you* believed the painting was a phoney we could never pass it off. That was why we couldn't let you know in advance. We needed you to come in cold.'

In a harsh voice she said, 'But you were going to expose me! Owen would have spoken about me to the press and everyone, and I'd have written about this splendid Moreno for the magazine. All the time you were lying, and deceiving me. You even asked about *craquelure* and detection methods. You pretended ignorance; you manipulated and exploited me–'

'Yes. But it wasn't meant to harm you.' She gave an angry laugh, and he said hurriedly, 'Wait, Claire. Please listen. It wouldn't have exposed and shamed you. Just think about it. Famous art critic, prominent New York artist, and talented young art historian engage in bold scheme to reveal just how phoney the New York art establishment has become, how they extol bad paintings just to be fashionable, how they promote the fraudulent and the inferior, how they regard art as little more than merchandise. How daring, how wild, how marvellous they might have seemed, this trio of campaigners, exposing the emperor's nakedness! Plenty of people would have admired our gall, doing this crazy thing and getting away with it. Owen would have sold the painting, yes, but then he'd have announced the truth, and given the buyer his money back, so no crime would have been committed. And you'd have written a different kind of article for *ArtDimension*, describing the whole scheme, how Owen and I chose the Echo and Narcissus myth for our subject because we wanted to illustrate the narcissism of the art world, and also how so many critics are as slavish as Echo, without an original voice. It would have been a sensational article, it would have made your name, you'd have become famous overnight, a brilliant writer and scholar...'

They stared at each other. 'All right,' she said, 'All right, I'm trying to understand. It might have seemed wicked and wonderful, as you say, and it might have enhanced my reputation rather than damage it, if I'd been the one to expose your game. But then why didn't you tell me? Why didn't you tell me the truth, at some point after I'd seen the painting?'

He continued gazing at her, and she looked back at him, regarding him, his face that she had come to know so well: those straight blue eyes; the fine nose and expressive mouth; the greying fair hair; and his hands which had painted the 'Echo and Narcissus'. Finally he said, 'I wanted to, but I kept delaying it. Suddenly it didn't seem amusing anymore, what we had done, not when I saw your bright enthusiastic face, looking at the painting, and when I felt your excitement. I began to have more and more misgivings, and to feel more and more afraid to tell you. And of course the more I delayed telling you the harder it became. Deceit, as we know, is like that, so insidious. You get tangled up in your own coils. You can lie out of cowardice or a failure of judgement, but if you come clean early enough you're usually forgiven. But if you're silenced by dread as I was, the deceit goes on and on and so does the fear... And I was doubting my own motives, becoming really dismayed about the whole business.' He moved his hands in a gesture of helplessness. '*ArtDimension* had given me a lousy mention in some review of Luke Reilly, and I began to suspect that maybe I had just been looking for revenge against the magazine, despite my pompous rationalisations about battling corruption in the art world. And some time ago you said you feared that loving me, and being so happy, might be a kind of *hubris*. But I realised soon enough that it was myself and Owen who had committed *hubris*, by playing around so much with people's feelings and even their reputations. Including yours. The feelings of a woman I'd begun to love. And then Owen was killed. It seemed a kind of judgement...'

She remained silent. Simon took a gulp of his beer, then went on in a low voice, 'And I lied to the police. Jesus, it was all becoming such a terrible web. But I believed that if I confessed to art forgery during Owen's murder investigation it would help no one, would only confuse things and might even implicate me in their eyes. So of course I lied. And now...' He stared at her, a stricken look on his face. 'And now it seems I've committed the perfect crime. I forged a painting, but your friend's pimp, or whatever he was, destroyed the evidence, so now nothing exists that could incriminate me. Only you and I know the truth, and from now on you and I will have to live with the knowledge that we are indeed implicated in Owen's murder. Not in the way the police might imagine, but, as far as I'm concerned, because of the crazy scheme in the first place, and, as far as you're concerned, because of your indiscretion with Zoë. And you know something? Both of us were under the influence of coke when we made our fatal mistakes, so maybe our story, in addition to everything else, is an indictment against that stuff, which happens to be the drug of choice in this fucked-up decade.'

Suddenly he clenched his fists on the table, and appealed to her gruffly, 'Claire! People aren't faultless. I was scared to tell you the truth partly because you idealise me so. I was afraid of what would happen when the idol toppled.'

She gave another hard laugh. 'Did I idealise you? I thought I just loved you.'

'You have to have a self to love somebody with. And your self, my sweetheart, is just forming.' He paused then said with emotion, 'But I do believe you love me. And because I love you as well I do truly want you to flourish. Despite your suspicions I would never have sabotaged your career. I want you to succeed, and I want the world to notice you for your true self, by which I mean your work, your talent, your spirit.'

Claire took a cautious swallow of her beer. She didn't know what she was feeling; all she knew was that everything seemed to be in turmoil. She was trying not to think too much, trying just to listen, to hear him, and she was also struggling not to cry. He continued, 'I often think of something you said to me that night you came to my loft after your evening out with Zoë, how you explained that your name, Claire Browne, means clarity and darkness, light and shadow. *Claire Obscure.*' He spread out his hands. 'The world, you know? Light and darkness. I am not saying that I didn't let my own darkness get out of hand. But won't you forgive me, Claire?'

Claire thought about how she had often suspected that the germ of some deep cynicism might be buried in her own idealism. And then there was Zoë, who trafficked in passion and dreams, and who was, in some ways, the bitterest cynic she'd ever known. She remembered the throng of Muslim men she had seen in Tompkins Park. Such an astonishing thing to glimpse from one's own bedroom window, on an ordinary New York morning, all those men in streaming robes, their chorusing prayer so harshly beautiful. She had thought then that there might be a lesson for her in such a vision, and now it occurred to her that the lesson was simple: the world has its own peculiar magic, or music, or madness. What a phoney *she* had been, living in her romantic cocoon!

Simon was still looking anxiously at her. She said, 'I don't know. I don't know what I am going to do now.'

He said hurriedly, 'There is something I want to ask you. Something I would like you to do, with me, that I think could be the solution for us.'

She stood up wearily. 'Ask me tomorrow. I will see you tomorrow. But now I'm going home.'

She began to move to the door, but a leaden sorrow was pressing on her, making the breath rasp in her throat. Suddenly everything in the world seemed false and empty. Simon came up beside her and placed his hand on her shoulder. 'Claire, will you come home with me tonight? I'm not asking you to decide anything right now. Just come home with me. You've been through too much pain to be alone tonight.'

Instead of answering she placed her face against his chest, and he put his arms around her.

# Epilogue

Next morning Claire left early, while Simon was still sleeping. Already the streets were a bath of heat. The downtown werewolves who had partied all night were only now emerging from the clubs, their finery crumpled, their faces grey in the sunlight. On Prince Street a girl was shouting at a scrawny young man. She had made herself up to look like a junkie – ragged hair, pallid face, black eyeshadow – but Claire reckoned she was too calculatedly dissipated-looking to be a real junkie. 'Don't give me that pseudo-downtown bullshit,' she was screaming at the skinny man, 'Don't give me that phoney, SoHo, East Village, TriBeCa, below-Fourteenth-Street downtown bullshit, know what I mean? *Do you know what I mean?*' Surprisingly, as Claire walked by, they both paused to dip her a courteous smile and say, 'Good morning,' before plunging back into their maelstrom.

Last night Simon had implored her to come away with him, to Ireland. 'Come with me. You don't want to live in this America. You want to live abroad, in Europe. You've told me so. Please come with me...'

He had been right; she did long to live in Europe. It had begun when she was a child, visiting Grandmother Fabienne in her dim apartment. They had walked together from room to room, hand-in-hand along the gloomy corridors, looking at Fabienne's oil paintings of Edwardian women, and her water-colours of Paris streets: trees shimmering with rain under a pearl sky, café tables, couples in evening dress hurrying along beneath black umbrellas, all the old-fashioned images of a *fin-de-siècle* boulevard. Grandmother Fabienne prepared plates of cheese and French bread, which they ate at her kitchen table with glasses of heavily watered wine, while Fabienne lectured:

'You must never eat like an American. They chop up all their meat into tiny bits, as if they were their own nanny, then they lay down the knife, and ferry up the food with their fork like a child. You must learn how to manage knife and fork with elegance, you must never eat fruit out of your hand as if you were a horse munching an apple, you must never tilt the soup plate towards you...'

She always took out the family albums so that Claire could marvel at her ancestors. And, oh, it was lovely, this glimpse of the exotic, the ancient and beautiful. Such a contrast to her unhappy home life. But those were happy days, herself and Fabienne in their own world in the dark apartment, drinking watered wine and looking down at sepia photographs, the grey head and the little auburn one almost touching. She had known that one day she would live in Europe – France, Spain,

England, even Ireland, perhaps. 'After all,' Fabienne had once said briskly to her, 'There is no reason you cannot choose a country. This is America; here we are used to people *choosing* a home, a place they weren't born in but which they make their own, through an effort of spirit or imagination, sometimes through love. There is no reason you also cannot become European, through love, by choice.'

So she would go. But she would not go with Simon.

The curious thing was that she did believe him. She believed that he did, had always, experienced their relationship as separate from the lies of the 'Echo' business. How he had achieved this split she didn't know, except to speculate that for a long time now he had been tangled up in self-deception. He had swallowed the values of this decade, he had changed his entire painting style, had whored after false muses and false gods, all in order to make it, and keep it, in New York. So perhaps it would not have been hard for him to evade the truth with regard to herself and the painting, perhaps it had been all too easy to cordon off one half of his mind and heart from the other half, to avert his eyes from the truth, since he was used to such evasions, such a flight. So she did, actually, believe him. She even believed that he did love her. Somehow, love had managed to break through his carapace of studied cool, somehow it had got in, got to his heart, despite himself.

*Being in love, she knew, was different from love.* All her life she had been her own enemy, carrying her mother in her bones. She had mistaken slight affairs for love, she had thought Jeremy could understand and redeem her, she had cheapened love, debased it by confusing it with romantic pipe dreams, with the fierce stimulations of physical pleasure. She'd had no faith.

She had expected far too much of the men with whom she'd involved herself. She had expected them to deliver her from her past, collude with her in her fantasies about herself, *rescue* her from herself. But she had been an atheist of love, so, of course, there had been no redemption, no release.

Without them she had no one, not even herself, since her knowledge of herself was too fragile, was still, in fact, in their hands... Did she want to go on like this forever, placing herself in other people's hands, asking them to expunge her history through some sentimental hocus-pocus, imploring them to re-create her so that she might, finally, love herself? She had been as oblivious as Narcissus, as silent as Echo. If she believed in love, she would have loved herself, she would have known she could be loved for herself, she would have loved Simon honestly.

London was close to Ireland; he could see her there, and she would visit him, at Ian Collins' house in West Cork, which, extraordinarily enough, was where her father's family came from, so she'd have gone there anyway. But she would not travel to Ireland with Simon. She would look after herself and write her book, which was what she should have been doing all along, as well as confronting her darkness, and looking for her own light.

The Old Masters did not often depict tenderness in love, except between Madonna and Child. They preferred fierce gods and swooning maidens, blazing goddesses and hapless mortal men, soldiers and Sabine women, general high drama. But Rembrandt captured tenderness, and intimacy, in 'The Jewish Bride'. She imagined him walking through Amsterdam's Jewish quarter, a familiar figure to the shopkeepers and children, who would look up from their coins and games to follow with their eyes this bulky, grizzled, tired-looking man who for some reason was inexorably drawn to them, to their Old Testament stories, to the glow of their Tabernacle lamp. The golden light of Rembrandt's palette had an Old Testament lustre, almost Oriental.

She thought of 'The Jewish Bride', that gentle couple, uncomfortable in their wedding clothes, so shy, so courteous, so young, so full of love. She sighed, glancing across Prince Street and noticing Fanelli's, which seemed open, despite the early hour. Without pausing she walked in.

Why was she entering a bar in the morning, when she was supposed to be going home? She supposed it had something to do with saying good bye to New York. Now that she'd decided to leave it, she wanted to offer it some homage, to praise the city she had loved. Those streets close to the Hudson River where the tall buildings dropped away and there were only cobblestones, warehouses, bars, and a blanched light – sea light – reminding you suddenly that Manhattan was an island. The old men hawking roasted chestnuts outside Radio City at Christmas, strolling through Central Park in autumn with her father. And places like Fanelli's, which never seemed to change.

The barman was drinking iced tea and reading *Variety*. 'Hi,' he said, 'Hot enough for you?'

Claire wondered if other people in other cities greeted one another with the heavily ironical *Hot enough for you?* on torrid summer days, or if this was a New York quirk.

She said, 'It must be eighty out there, already. Why don't you turn on the air conditioner?'

'It's broken. That's why I'm open so early; the repair guy's supposed to come. Want an iced tea?'

'Thank you.' She settled at the bar, and touched his magazine. 'Are you an actor?'

'Who isn't?' He gave her the iced tea, which was decorated with a crescent of lemon and a mint leaf. She drank it thirstily, and said, 'I'm going to England, to live. Did you know that in England they loathe the very idea of iced tea? They think it's an American aberration.'

'Yeah?' He regarded his own glass. 'If it was as hot over there as it is in this town I bet they'd learn to like iced tea pretty fast.'

With a prickle of alarm Claire suddenly registered that she and the barman were not alone. Another man was slumped at a table in the corner, a big, dishevelled man with grey hair, a ruined face, and pale eyes which were staring foggily at her.

The barman said, 'Don't mind him. He was so blasted last night at closing time, they let him stay to sleep it off, since he's a regular. He was here when I came in, still sleeping. I'll get him a coffee in a while. He probably doesn't know where he is, poor bastard.'

Claire said, 'I think I've seen him before, at Roy's. He's German, isn't he?'

'He's always around. An art collector or something. He gets plastered and foams at the mouth, screaming at anyone who'll listen about how shitty the art world has become. Well, he buys the booze, so people pretend they agree, you know. But it only encourages him, bitter old fucker.'

The man at the table gave a derisive snort, as though aware he was being talked about, then his head fell heavily down on the table.

\* \* \*

At the border of SoHo and the Village, she came across a church she had never noticed before, Roman Catholic in the pseudo-Gothic style, with solemn stone figures adorning the portal; it was called Saint Catherine's. As with Fanelli's, she was surprised to find it open.

How dark it was, and cool, with panels of vaporous light sloping in through the windows, to gild the pews and the stone floor. She dipped her fingers into the font and blessed herself. The water was cold and smelled of must.

Slowly she moved along the church, through the dimness and the panels of radiant smoke, gazing at the coloured glass, the rose window, the stations of the cross, the paintings. She was alone.

There was a picture, in one of the chapels, which intrigued her because she could not place its theme. It must be a moment from the life of a saint, she said to herself, but I do not know it. It was painted in the Baroque manner, and showed a woman in a bed, startled out of sleep by the visit of an angel. The bed was lavish, with a crimson canopy, and tousled clothes of crimson and gold. The woman was wearing a demure nightdress, ivory-coloured, with long sleeves; she had an abundance of red-gold hair. Her mouth was open, revealing a gleam of teeth, and her eyes stared in wonderment at the angel, who was hovering just above the floor, at the foot of the bed. He was a nice-looking angel, golden-haired in the traditional way, with golden slippers on his little, suspended feet. He had a rather Plantagenet face, slender and fine, and his hands, also fine, were extended to the girl as if to implore her not to be alarmed. His stiff robe resembled her nightdress, and he had enormous, clumsily painted wings. On a table by the bed were a gold cup, a prayer book, a candle, and a fresh red rose.

Claire felt a sob rise in her throat, which she managed to suppress. She thought about the day unfurling ahead of her, how lonely she would be. Like the days before Simon, her apartment dry and empty, the people in the streets going about their own business, the vulnerability one feels, without love to protect and sustain one, that warmth at the centre of the spirit. She could call Simon now, she could forget her pride. She could lose herself once again in his arms.

She heard the creak of a leather shoe, and turning, saw a priest, a slight youngish man with russet hair – her first, uneasy thought was that he resembled Zoë's Lloyd. He came up beside her and said in an Irish accent, 'I always draw spiritual consolation from this painting, I don't know why.'

'What is the subject?' she asked.

He laughed. 'I've no idea, though it reminds me of that poem by Keats, "The Eve of Saint Agnes". Do you know it? The lady's bower awash with moonlight, the lady herself in bed asleep, dreaming of love, and the young man who plays the lute until,' the priest cleared his throat, '"Her blue affrayed eyes wide open shone..." And then they go off, together.' He laughed again. 'As I say, I don't know why this picture consoles me, since its subject strikes me as literary rather than religious, despite the angel.'

'He seems a nice angel,' Claire ventured, 'with his two little feet.'

'Yes, a solicitous angel, a bit anxious for the girl. Perhaps I like the painting because it reminds me that men and women, human beings, can sustain all kinds of connections beyond the obvious kind such as the sexual tug between lovers, or the connection between parent and child, or priest and parishioner.' He gestured to the painting. 'It isn't clear who the lady is. She

232

could be a saint but I cannot identify her, and she hasn't a halo. She seems to be just a young woman in a bed, and the angel seems just to care for her.'

Claire said slowly, 'I see what you mean. It's obviously not an Annunciation, although it resembles one, with the angel and startled maiden. It's as though the painting is trying to describe a spiritual connection between these two characters which extends beyond the *literally* religious, but which isn't sexual, either.'

'Exactly. There is a sense of mystery about it which you have just helped me to define. Maybe he is her guardian angel, who is worried about her. In Ireland, as children, we were told that we each had a guardian angel, but I haven't ever seen mine. It was said to us that when we did something naughty, our guardian angel put his head under his wing, and cried.'

They gazed at the painting in silence for a moment. Suddenly Claire asked, 'What would you do, if you were betrayed by someone you loved?'

He gave her an intent look. 'I would be compelled to follow the example of Christ.'

'You mean, you would forgive the person?' She was surprised by the waspishness in her voice.

'I suppose that sounds trite to you, and simplistic? Well, we are all human... Do you love this person, still?'

'Yes,' she answered quietly, 'Yes, I think I do.'

Again he regarded the painting. 'It sounds as though one of the strands in your relationship with this person – perhaps the spiritual strand – has been torn. One of the ways of caring has been damaged. That is why you are feeling wounded. There is a wound in the relationship, at one of its important levels.'

'Do you think – can that kind of damage be repaired?'

'Yes,' he answered soberly, 'I would say so, if you believe in grace.' He smiled at her, a warm smile, and she realised that he didn't look remotely like Lloyd, after all. 'Of course, the grace must illuminate your life from within. It must flow from your own source.'

'You are saying that one must love oneself?' She paused. 'Often I am – uncertain, and afraid, and I can't feel a place in myself which might be loveable.' Again, she paused, but when she registered that he was listening closely to her, his eyes narrowed in concentration, she continued, 'At moments like this, though, when I am feeling what you might call a *heart* connection to someone, when my mind and heart seem to be engaged, then I think I love myself. And when I am working, really *working*, when I'm looking carefully at paintings, and writing, then it's as though I am touching the place in myself which is true, the place where I can love myself. I do love myself in that place.'

He answered in his serious voice, 'I feel a heart connection to you, as well. I cannot remember the last time I spontaneously quoted poetry, but with you I was babbling my bit of Keats quite naturally. It felt very nice.'

'Irish people are lovely at that kind of thing, glorying in words and so on. My family are from West Cork. I intend to go there, to live. I will be studying in London for a year, and then I think I won't return to America. I will go to Ireland.'

'My people are from County Cavan. My father is an O'Reilly and my mother is a Brady. You can't get more Cavan than that.' He blushed, suddenly, and Claire realised he was much younger than she'd thought, younger than herself.

'This man,' she said impulsively, 'this man who betrayed me. He is called Brady, too.' She felt obliged to continue, 'He didn't betray me in the *usual* way. It wasn't a *woman*, that kind of thing...' Abashed, also blushing, she fell silent.

The priest examined his sleeve. 'There is a teaching, about Judas, who betrayed Christ. It is an heretical teaching, so I cannot – I must not – espouse it as doctrine. But as a story, a philosophical sort of story, it might interest you.' He looked up, smiling. 'According to this teaching, Judas is a saint, because Christ *had* to be betrayed, so that He could fulfil his purpose on earth, and thereby redeem us all. So someone *had* to betray Him. And Judas bravely took on this role, even though he knew that he would never be loved and honoured, like the other saints, but only vilified, for all time.'

'Betrayal is necessary?' asked Claire.

'It made something possible,' he answered, 'Something good.'

* * *

Walking home, she considered what she would do that day: write to the Courtauld, accepting their grant, work on her book, call Cecily. And call Simon. She would invite him to dinner, she decided, later in the week. It would be hot in her apartment but she would prepare a cold supper, perhaps cold salmon, with home-made mayonnaise, and a cucumber salad. And he would bring a bottle of white wine.

He would see her flat for the first time; he would walk in tentatively, bearing his gift of white wine, and she would feel awkward also, nervous about the heat of the evening, about her small apartment and modest furniture. But she would have bought fresh flowers to decorate the table, and she would wear a light dress with a pattern of flowers. Almost shyly, Simon would place the bottle in her hands – the paper sheathing it would have grown wilted and damp with the heat.

They would kiss as friends. And presently they would talk about the future, his journey to the west of Ireland and hers to London, how they might meet, one or the other of them crossing the Irish Sea. They would eat the food and drink the wine. Slowly they would relax.

Perhaps it would be a new beginning.

## Also by Elizabeth Wassell

# The Honey Plain

*'If you behave like a bastard, you turn women into bitches!'*

Dermot O'Duffy has a reputation as a philanderer.
His marriage to the flame-haired Fiona is foundering.

Then along comes Grania — a young painter who challenges
his antics — and together they embark on a rollicking affair
around Ireland, just one step ahead of a posse including Fiona,
her angry father and an oily popinjay called Doyle.

Fast-paced, funny and vivid, Elizabeth Wassell's first novel is
a memorable quest for love in our cynical times.

'In *The Honey Plain* Elizabeth Wassell has written a realistic
novel with a mythological presence; a satiric-comic novel
with a serious feel; and a rattling good yarn bristling with ideas.
Essentially, though, *The Honey Plain* is a touching love story,
well wrought and well told.'
*Brendan Kennelly*

ISBN 0-86327-595-8

WOLFHOUND PRESS
68 Mountjoy Square, Dublin 1

## Also from Wolfhound Press

# Celtic Fury

## by Seán Kenny

*Jack Amonson was once a successful thriller writer.
Now he lives in Guadalajara, Mexico, tormented by memories
and dreams of the past. Seventeen years have gone by,
but each day he must live through those events again....*

At the height of his success, Jack and his actress wife, Maeve,
move to her home village of Rathbrack in the west of Ireland.

Very much in love, expecting their first child, and planning
their dream home — their future happiness seems assured.
But the land on which they lay the foundations is not really
theirs to build on, and before long, bizarre and sinister events
begin to occur in the village.

Who are the old beggar Fortycoats
and the incredibly beautiful Áine?

The author of *The Hungry Earth* once again blends
supernatural occurrences and sexual intrigue in a story that
searches out the heart of the Irish condition — a tale that will
linger in your mind long after the last line....

ISBN 0-86327-607-5

*Also from Wolfhound Press*

# Tribe

## by John F. McDonald

*'... Ann's out there in the puke world systemising and synchronising. Tom Lee and Tolui ... is praying to their horse god for Monday to come round.... And pretty Peggy lies here wrapped in a blanket in front of the fire.*
*Still — don't think I'm complaining.'*

Another Friday night for Owen McBride. The beginning of a year of indecision. Time to make a choice.

Poised between two worlds — a foot in each — Owen must step across the line. Traveller or *Gorgio*. Who is he?

And as the year progresses, can either existence provide sanctuary from the Manchester underworld in which he unwittingly becomes entangled?

*Tribe* is John F. McDonald's cutting-edge look at society at the end of the 1990s, through the eyes of Owen McBride — a man torn between an untethered existence and the caged respectability of his girlfriend's dreams.

ISBN 0-86327-720-9